1st ed   OP

EAGLE IN THE AIR

A Novel by
Rose Robinson

CROWN PUBLISHERS, INC. New York

To my sisters,
Adrienne and Bernice

There be three things
which are too wonderful to me,
yea, four, which I know not:
The way of an eagle in the air;
the way of a serpent upon the rock;
the way of a ship in the midst
of the sea;
and the way of a man with a maid.

PROVERBS 30 : 18, 19

Chapter One

"Jeannie . . . Jeannie Pierce! Hey, pretty brown girl!"
  "What, honey?"
  "Anything important coming over the radio?"
  "Uh-huh. They're sending the cops."
  "Hey, cops, everybody."
  "Say how many?"
  "Yes. Three thousand."
  "Damn!"
  "And they've got shotguns and clubs and tear gas."
  "What do they think this is, Vietnam?"
  "Three thousand for two hundred students?"
  "Aw man, they think big here in Chicago."
  "Turn it up, Jeannie."
  "—holding the Midwestern University Administration Building for two days. Dr. Bauer, the president, is still locked up in his office."
  "Three thousand cops."
  "Listen."
  "—Armored cars, and buses—"
  "Maybe this is Vietnam."

"Quiet, Freeman."

"—Mayor Moony said, and I quote, 'Flush them out by any means possible.' "

"Hey, why don't they give our side?"

"Hold it. He's telling where they are."

"—a square mile from Cottage Grove to Stony Island and from 71st to 79th—"

Smack! "Not on the wall, man."

"Can't sit still with all these mosquitoes eating me up. Where'd they come from this time of year?"

"I'm hot. Somebody open a window."

"—have presented their grievances—"

"Open a window, Jeannie."

"Hang on, hear?"

"—not enough student representation, unfit food in cafeterias, no recreation for ghetto children—"

"Let's sing something."

"What time is it?"

"Two thirteen aye em."

"Jeannie, open the window. It's stuffy in here."

"In a minute."

"Jeannie, you beautiful thing you."

"Okay." *Rumble scrooch.*

"See, y'got to talk nice to 'em or they won't do nothin' for ya."

"Hey, everybody, let's sing."

Swat! Swat swat! "Look out Freeman, that's me, man."

"Sorry 'bout that." *Swat swat!*

" 'Michael, row the boat ashore—' "

"Maybe we ought to let Dr. Bauer go."

"No. Long's we've got him, they won't do anything drastic."

" 'Ah-lay-looo-yah.' Sing, somebody, won't you? I don't want to solo."

10

"Don't count on me, Linda. I can't sing."

"Come on, everybody. 'Mi-cul rowww—' "

"They want us to give up—"

" '—ashore ah-lay-' "

"No deals. We've gone this far." *Swat. Swatswatswat.*

"Cut it out, man. 'S too crowded to be beating the air like that."

"Can't stand 'em." Swat. "Got 'im."

"Sing *any*body . . . You'll feel better."

"Achoo. Achoo . . . Aaaaaahhhhchoo achoo *Achoo!*"

"Put the window down some, Jeannie—"

"Hold it. I'm listening."

"Achoo. Aaa—*choo.* Achoo achoo—"

"Aw, hell."

"Don't be so jumpy. This is not the time to get our backs up."

" 'Michael, row'—sing, someone please—"

" 'The boat ashore hah-lay-loo-' " *Clap clap*

"Feel better, baby, now that they're making some noise and I can't hear the radio?"

"Achooooo. Aaaaaaaaaaah—*chooooo!*"

"Oh, f'Chrissake."

"Jeannie?"

"Wait . . . Ohhhh, goodness!"

"What's up, Jeannie?"

"They've got helicopters too."

"I know. They're gonna bomb us, that's what. Give me a piece of paper so I can make out my will."

"This's no time for levity, kids. And remember, we've got to keep this thing nonviolent. Don't give them any excuses."

"Aaaachoo achoooooo aaaaaaaaaachooooooooooo!"

"Say, can anybody get near that window besides Jeannie without killing someone?"

"Okay, I'll fix it. Jerry, hold my radio." *Scrunch.* "That better?" *Sniff snoff.* "Yes."

" '—Chilly and wide—' " *Clap*—" 'Lay-loo-' " *Clap clap.*

"Remember your instructions. Don't give 'em any excuses to shoot."

" 'Milk and honey on the other side—' "

"Aw, they won't shoot."

"Never know with three thousand hotheads."

"We're sitting ducks."

"Well, I'm damned if I'm going to stand 'til they get here."

"Why don't you sing, Freeman? You'll feel better."

"Can't sing, I told you."

" 'Michael, row the boat ashore—' "

"Oh, relax. They know we're not a mob."

"Yeah? Well, what about those stupids broke those windows and all that furniture?"

"But we didn't hurt anybody."

"Just kidnapped God in there. Maybe we ought to let him go."

"Ah, take it easy."

"Jeannie?"

"Yep?"

"See anything on your side?"

"Nope. I'll let you know."

"Anybody see anything outside?"

"Not a thing."

"Uh-uh."

"Just lights, and trees bending like crazy."

"Nothing but night over here."

"The phone's ringing. Don, answer it."

" 'Freedom's waters—' "

"Hey, stop singing for a while. Hello."

"Who is it?"

"Just a minute, sir. Dr. Meyers. The chancellor. Says they'll give us fifteen minutes to clear out and release Dr. Bauer unharmed, and they won't use force if we say the word now."

"Nothing doing!"

"They haven't met our demands, so we're not coming out. Tell him that."

"That how all of you feel?"

"Yes!"

"Hey, I was across the hall, heard the phone ring. Who is it?"

"The chancellor. Wants us to give in. You guys over there for that?"

"Very thing we were talking about. Naw, no man."

"Dr. Meyers? Sorry, we're staying here." *Click!*

"Karen, keep your cool, hear?"

"I'm trying. I really am."

"You're getting yourself all worked up . . . It's not like you're alone. We're in this together."

"That gives me great comfort."

"You can always leave."

"And look like a coward in front of everyone?"

" 'Michael, row—' "

"Sing something else."

"Can't think of anything but that."

"How about 'We Shall Overcome'? 'We shaaaalll—' " Ovurr-cahhhh-ah-um.' "

"Clubs and tear gas and shotguns?"

" 'Weeee shaaaallll owe-verrrrcaaaah-ah-ahm.' "

"Here come the cops!"

"Hold it! Jeannie says they're coming."

"Good Lord!"

"I see armored tanks and squad cars."

"Why do they have to use those blasted bright lights?"

"And sirens."

"They're pouring out and attaching bayonets."

"Better turn this thing off. No point listening now."

"Ooohh, what're they going to do?"

"T-take it easy, hear? G-get hold of yourself, D-Doris."

"You have two minutes to come out!"

"Don't hold my hand. I can't think when someone's holding on to me."

"We mean business!"

"But I've got to hold something."

"Then grab the desk leg."

Close your mouth, Jean Pierce. Darn! Everyone looks scared. Keep calm now. "I said come out! . . . . One minute!" God help us. Don't lose your head, Jeannie. "Your time's up! Turn those lights on the door!" Ferris warned you. He told you not to.

"They're coming. I can hear them downstairs."

"Wonder what the kids in the other rooms are doing?"

"Should've asked Bill while he was here. Anyway, can't worry about them now. And remember, don't retaliate."

"They're out in the hall."

"All right, men. Take them any way you can!"

14

Chapter Two

The demonstrators were clubbed off to jail and jammed in, six to a cell. Jean Pierce had a bruise on her leg. Not a bad one. Like everyone else, she stank and hurt, hating the police, the chancellor, the mayor. Some of the other girls were crying, those who'd been beaten more than she and then dragged feetfirst downstairs. Their sad waves washed up, "bail, trials, lawyers," while, dry-eyed and introspective, Jean only wondered when she'd get out. Because every minute was a month.

Ferris had told her to stay out of the mess. Said she didn't know what the hell she was getting into. He'd been rough, going straight to the point. Now she understood. She guessed he'd heard what happened. And how long would it be before she saw him again? If there was a trial, would he come? He liked her, she was sure of that, but wasn't sure how much. One thing she knew. She missed him.

And she missed her radio, a wrecked thing, thrown away. Her sister had given it to her for Christmas. Half-sister really. She'd just had a miscarriage and hadn't been at all well. It was her nerves mostly. This business would be in the papers back in Des Graces, a little town foundering in Iowa. And Chris would read

15

all about it and worry herself sicker. Over the phone Jean had let it out she'd be taking part in it. And Chris hadn't been too happy about that.

Daylight showed through a high inviolable window, slowly increased. The opprobrious slumped against the walls or flopped on the floor. There weren't any chairs and only one foul cot. Their crying turned into sniffles, into damp questions sent flying after will-o'-the-wisp answers. When would they be taken to court? And what kind of judge would they get? Hard or soft? Or was there any such thing as a soft judge? Were all of them to be tried at once? So many unnecessary questions.

Considering before noon they were free. Evicted by an unmotherly matron. Jean rode an elevator down to a large room clogged with the newly emancipated and a legion of police. The ex-prisoners were terribly joyful. On the other side of a low wooden barrier were parents and friends come to sort out their own. The inner swell fed the outer one, knotting here and there for affection or antiseptic pacts.

Seeing all that, it came to Jean she was miles from the dorm and didn't have any money. And then someone called out, "Jeannie!" A man who was dark brown and crinkly haired, exceptionally handsome and tall.

She said, "Ferris!" And pressed between people and beyond a low swinging gate. He told her he'd been there since five that morning, showing anger under his thick brows and full moustache, and put his arm around her erotic slenderness and steered her out to his late-model black sedan. Had they hurt her? She said, "Not really," He'd heard everything on his radio, and after that, had called the warden's office. Turning the key in the ignition, he said he was going to take her to a restaurant. "Not 'til I've had a shower," she answered. Her stretch pants and sweater had dried mud on the backs.

"Okay," he grumbled. She could see he was tired. "Couldn't sleep last night, dammit, worrying about you. I knew something like this was gonna happen. That's why I told you not to get mixed up in this thing."

"It seemed important," she whispered.

He licked film onto his full lower lip. "Important, hell. Suppose you'd ended up in the hospital like some of 'em did?" He told her not to do it again, and she promised she wouldn't. Not this year, not next. Next time someone else could do it. She'd had her turn.

He powered away from the long gray building. And leaving it, Jean felt easier. When he had to wait on signal he took her by the shoulder and kissed her lightly on the lips. "You're hardheaded, y' know that?" he asked, less angry.

Smiling, she dodged. "I'm so glad to see you," and put her head on his arm.

Playfully, he flattened her nose with his thumb. The light turned green. He drove her to the front of the dorm. Suddenly she was too tired for breakfast, and yawning, thought she'd take a nap. "Okay," he told her. "call me later. I'll be home," and let her out of his car.

Before she went in, she watched it course down the shaded street. Then pushing glass in a half circle, she crossed tile to the service desk and smiled at the woman behind it. The woman, who was short and middle-aged, looked up from a pile of receipts. They'd known each other for nearly three years and had always been on good terms. Jean said, "Hi, Mrs. McNulty," and asked for her key.

Piloting instant wrinkles, Mrs. McNulty went to a wall board that was off to one side and took down 507, and coming back, told Jean she was to get her things out of the room. The girl said she didn't understand, so Mrs. McNulty said it again. And all

Jean got for trying to force an explanation was, "Call the Administration Building on Monday. I'm sure you know where it is."

Jean's voice cracked out of the shell of her throat. "Do I have time for a shower?"

"Of course," the woman said coldly.

Jean didn't ride the elevator but walked upstairs instead because she didn't want anyone to see her just then. Five floors higher in her cubicle she cried softly for everything that was going to waste. All her hard work, tests suffered, headaches from staying up nights, years of fun missed, fears and anxious times— all blown up. That's why there hadn't been any trial. The school administrators had held their own. It was crazy. They couldn't just say they didn't want her around anymore. Two days setting fire to nearly three years? Crazy, crazy, crazy!

Half drained, she went into the bathroom and made the spray fall on her as hot as she could stand it. Later, while she was drying herself, the phone rang. Naked and dreary, she answered it. Mrs. McNulty wanted to know how long she'd be. She guessed bitterly, "About an hour," then asked for an outside number, waited, heard a buzz, dialing, three rings.

Ferris said, "Hello."

"Honey, I've been expelled," Jean told him. "From school, from the dorm."

He said, "Damn!" and for a second nothing, then, "How much time have you got?"

"Less than an hour," she answered.

He promised he'd be right over and take her to his place.

Trembling, she said, "I—I need boxes."

He wondered how many. She made a reasonable estimate. "Okay," he said, "I'll see you."

In a few minutes, he was in the lobby. Some of the girls on her floor helped her take everything down because men weren't allowed upstairs. They'd seen her tottering over to the elevator and asked if she was moving, and heard why. They all said they were sorry, and hoped things could be worked out.

The outcast's sum total was piled in the trunk and rear seat of Ferris' sedan. Before they'd gone a block Jean said hollowly, "I won't be on your hands long. Until I call my sister." She wore a dress now, short, yellow, half-hidden by a bulky sweater. It was crisp outside and windy. Her hair made a long black tail behind her. Then she whispered something about trying for reinstatement, not sounding optimistic.

He said, "You can try—"

"But what?" Just that on the way over, the radio said all expulsions were final. Then seeing how she looked, he said the report could be wrong.

But still, if it weren't, she would lose the scholarship she'd got, not for being lucid but poor and at least apt. A poverty dole, she called it. Because when she was a little girl her mother got a divorce from her father. Jean didn't remember him. And because her mother had done domestic work until sickness forced her on welfare. Last year she died of cancer. Jean mentioned that, showing strain, suddenly very tired.

He said, "It's not the end of the world."

"Time I'm finished," she shuddered, "it will be." Going straight to the point, he asked about the money situation. Back in the dorm she had counted what she had. Four dollars and fifty-three cents. "Fine," she whispered.

He said, "You're a liar."

"I was supposed to get my monthly expense check," she admitted, knowing that now there wouldn't be any.

His car cruised west, encountering traffic, going by trees. Apartment buildings were dense on the street where Ferris parked, and the neighborhood was well kept. He helped her carry her belongings up two flights of stairs for as many trips as it took. Feeling awful, holding it in, Jean called Des Graces but didn't get any answer. She said she'd try again later. Ferris was sitting on the couch. He'd loosened his tie and hung his gray suit jacket down beside him. Off and on he did nervous things. And flaring his nostrils he said, "You got plenty time." Matter of fact she didn't have to go to Des Graces. What was there, anyway?

She could have told him bigotry and a broom. A chance to be humble. Set someone else's house in order. That much. And be snubbed by most of the light foks because she was dark, and by most of the dark folks because she'd been to college. All the people who were broom sweepers and humble through sundown on Saturday. They'd swept up fairly nice homes of their own and shared a faith that paraded clothes and burned mortages on Sunday. She could have told Ferris. But she already had and he remembered. "Everything I get into blows up," she said. "I'm a loser." He said she wasn't. She was sitting on one arm of the couch facing away from him. All at once she got up and walked slowly around the large room that hadn't much furniture and needed dusting. "I must be," she sighed.

He enjoyed her face that was a shade lighter than his own, the high cheekbones, slanted eyes, and straight nose, and he watched the graceful way she touched a chair. "Stop knocking yourself down," he told her. "And going back to that one-horse town don't make no kinda sense. You're not the kinda chick could put up with that stuff. . . . Anyone back there?"

"No," she answered, "I'd have told you."

Feeling better, he stretched his legs and made his thigh muscles work. "Well, nobody there, what's the rush?"

She frowned, "There isn't anything else—if they don't let me back in school."

"Get a job here."

"You make it sound so easy. Who says I'd get one right away? And what would I live on until then? I haven't any money, don't know anybody."

"You know me," he said, setting his brown eyes on her.

"Oh, honey, I don't want to."

"Don't want to what?"

"Borrow from you."

"What's wrong with that? You know you're not just anybody. Been thinkin' about you a lot lately." Ever since he'd met her at the party three weeks ago that she'd almost bypassed because of so much homework. For most of the night they danced or talked with each other. And then he took her home. Now he wasn't dating anyone else. "I'm asking you, what's wrong?"

"I didn't say anything was. I just don't want to."

"Well, tell me something. If you don't have but four dollars and some odd cents, how the hell you gonna get back to Iowa?" She told him about the return bus ticket that was in her purse. Something she always bought ahead of time so she wouldn't overspend. Locking his strong fingers behind his head, he let go of a one-note laugh. "Y' know, you're pretty independent, babe?" She put her head down in a soft way, showing lovely white teeth. "Hey, let's eat. You gotta be hungry." She said she wasn't. "Did you buy lunch?"

"No."

"Then you're hungry," he decided, springing up.

He wouldn't let her help with the meal. Said she should rest. She waited in the living room where the floors were hardwood and the wallpaper pale tan. The large rug needed cleaning. One wide window faced front and east and a smaller one let in light from the north. There were blinds but no curtains or draperies.

That room claimed a few lamps, small tables, two upholstered chairs, a television set, the couch. Not much else.

Ferris fixed a good meal, and she found out she was starved. She ate in a hurry, finished before he did, and buzzed Des Graces again. It didn't hear her. "Oh, this is awful," she said, putting the phone down. He had been gazing off into space, hearing the phone pleading. Now he looked at her hard. "I can't get them. What am I going to do?" she asked him.

He said, "Wait. Nothing else you can do. No use worrying about it." And then he told her, "I know what you need."

She asked, "What?"

"Just a sec." Forcing her to her feet, he crutched her unresisting to his bedroom, and went out closing the door behind him. She sagged onto coarse dark blue without remembering when she lay down.

Chapter Three

Ferris Boone wasn't a humble man. He had a hard side and didn't like giving away anything for nothing. He was complex and believed in defending himself in ways learned on the corner where he grew up in Chicago.

Jean knew he'd been married before. For six years and separated for two. His wife bought the divorce and got another husband. There were no children. Ferris swore on a bottle he'd never marry again.

His ex-wife had a master's degree, and down at the tavern he usually brought that up, keeping it quiet that he'd dropped out after three years of high school. He dated only college women, and not counting degrees, a good many.

He was thirty-two years old, twelve years older than Jean.

After he crutched her to his bedroom, he took off his shirt and got out a carton of beer. Then he turned on the television set and sat on the couch, all the time thinking about her. The way she showed all her feelings. And a lot more. He wondered if she'd taken off her clothes, and how her body looked. Great, he guessed, with the shape she had. No other girl in the world had a shape like Jeannie's.

The big dark man shook suds. And some of it flowed down to the coffee table when he set his can on the leather top and braced the back of his head in his hands. His pulse came up to his skin. "Nobody." He glanced at the clock on the wall. She hadn't been sleeping long. His broad blunt jaw moved. He felt giddy, raised one leg, the other, tapped his toes. Got up, walked around. Ate supper. Drank another beer. Looked out the kitchen window at flowers coming up along the rear fence.

Finally he returned to the couch, spread his wings on the back, and stared down the channel between his legs. He didn't have any idea what program was playing, especially with the sound turned low. When it struck him he was in the dark, he turned on the lamp on a table next to the couch and made a little light. The ring of the phone was a shock. A woman he used to date wondered where he'd been. He talked with her for a while without making any promises.

Jean woke up in blackness and wondered what time it was. A sluggish flash of her sister came. She ought to be home, or anyway Bernie. She struggled up, let her arms lengthen her body, sagged back to what was normal for the moment, and opened the door. She looked past Ferris' back at the two men on the TV screen shoving each other. "You didn't have to keep it low," she yawned.

He shrugged with a can of beer in his hand and went over and raised the volume, asking her, "How'd you sleep?"

" 'Kay, I guess," she yawned again.

"Haven't had enough," he said.

She worked a crick out of her neck. "Guess not. But I'll call Chris first. What time is it?"

"Nine thirty."

"Whaat?" She saw the clock then. "You mean I've been out six hours?"

24

"Just about."

"Didn't seem like it." She walked over to the phone on the lamp table. "Well, let's hope."

"What if she's not there?"

She said, "She's got to be." And Ferris' hand twitched. He frowned and looked the other way. The phone rang eight times before she said, "Hi, Bernie. Where's Chris?" And then listened while Ferris cornered a squint at the dreadful look on her face.

Bernie was Chris's husband. He said Jean knew how his wife had been. "Acting strange and everything." Well, since the last time Jean had called, a couple of weeks ago, Chris wasn't making out too good. She'd had a breakdown. They just took her to the hospital. She didn't know anyone. Not even him. He said he was staying at his mother's for a while, closing up his house. The doctor ruled out visitors right off.

"Anything I can do?" Jean asked. She was shaking.

And heard, "Not just now." He'd let her know later on.

"Okay, Bernie," she told him. "I better call you, hear? Bye." She put the phone back where it belonged and held on for dear life.

"Something wrong?" asked Ferris, knowing that everything was.

She panted, "Can I sleep here tonight?"

"You don't have to ask," he told her, shaking his beer, then pulled, "What did he say?"

She walked slowly, passing behind him, going to the other end of the couch and sitting down. "They've got to let me in again," she whispered.

"Tell me what he said."

"I *need* it."

"Honey, look," he frowned, "talk it out. You'll feel better."

She sighed dismally, "That was my brother-in-law," and told him the rest.

"Damn shame," he groaned and drank a little brew.

"Why'd it have to be Chris?" she asked nobody at all, putting her head back.

His eyes poised on her throat, skied the hill, and landed in her lap. Under his armpits he was sweating and sweat ran down his back. He whispered, "Could happen to anyone, sweets."

And Jean said, "But she was so perfect."

"What's perfect?" he asked. "Tell me."

"Tiny, dainty," she said. "Everyone liked her. She was beautiful."

"You're beautiful," he smiled. "What d'you mean?"

"No," she wrinkled her forehead, "I mean what people back home call beautiful." Chris was light with long, brown, silky hair and hazel eyes. She was five feet tall, four inches shorter than Jean and eight years older. They didn't resemble each other. Chris had a different father and looked like him. She'd been incredibly popular. Jean looked up to her. The man Chris had married was light and good-looking and had large smooth waves in his hair. Five days a week he kept one of the grammar schools clean. That was considered a good job. They were a fine match, Crystal and Bernard Bennett. "I had a crush on him when I was eleven," Jean remembered. "He used to laugh about that. Oh, my sister's had so much trouble. Losing her first baby—" after ten years of panicky struggle. "And now—why does it have to be like this?" Ferris knew she was talking about herself now and feeling guilty that she was. Her head began to hurt.

He said, "Come on over here and sit down," touching the cushion near him with his beer can. She moved over and he put his arms around her, saying, "Let it out, babe." And then she did.

26

"That's right, that's it." He kissed her gently. And for a while her head stopped hurting.

"I—I'll pay you for the phone call," she whimpered.

"What? Don't be silly," he whispered.

She said, "You're doing enough for me."

"I said forget it," he sent back . . . "How d'you feel?"

"Better."

"Want to stay up or go to bed?"

"Think I'll get some more sleep," she said, squirming. "Let me take the couch. It's 'way too short for you."

"No, it's not, babe," he said, grinning. "It's one of those convertible jobs, so don't worry about it." With that he picked her up and carried her across the room to the one with the bed in it.

"I need my things," she told him.

"Coming right up," he promised and set her down on the soft raft, made light, and went away to the living-room closet.

She called out, "Just my overnight bag." He found it while she watched his body curve, then straighten, saw the marvelous strain in his upper arm lugging the load. He set it down next to the bed. "We keep going over the same scene." She tried to smile.

"Well, you didn't get much sleep the last two nights," he said, trying to sound casual, tight as his throat felt. It moved and his nostrils flared. He pressed his lips against his teeth. "See you in the morning."

"You going to bed right away?" she wanted to know.

"Might stay up and catch the late show."

"Okay . . . see you, hon."

Almost as soon as he closed the door her headache came back. At first it was only a small dull ache behind one ear. She told herself, I'll feel better in the morning, and opened her bag, took out shortie pajamas and a short matching robe and slippers. She made herself naked. Saw her body in the closet-door mirror. Her full rounded breasts arching high, small waist, her hips swelling down to full thighs, full calves, small nervous feet. The pink pajamas didn't conceal her very much. Their hem ruffled at her hipline. She heard Ferris outside the door walking, walking, and wondered why he was. Her head ached worse than before. She sat on a chair near the only window. Ferris was a strong man, warm. She heard him again. And then she couldn't hear him, and listened for him.

The bedroom light hadn't gone out. Ferris could see it under the door. Jean had left him over an hour ago. And he was getting more tense, and all heated up, and trying to walk it off. That didn't do any good. He thought about knocking on the door and telling her to come out and then holding her in his arms again. Because he wanted her, yeah he wanted her, wanted her. Okay, so she'd be there tomorrow and maybe for longer than that. But tonight was what was tearing him up. Sure he could knock. Think of something to say. Say he'd forgot—what?

Agitated, he plopped down again. Heard a noise. Jumped, turning around. Pale light polished his muscles. He raised to one knee. "Thought you were sleeping," he said. She was wearing her robe. He stared at her legs.

"Got any aspirin?" she murmured. "For my headache."

He said, "Just a minute," and went into the bathroom and made a small commotion, shoving bottles and boxes while she took the place he'd left warm. Coming back, "Here y' go."—he handed her a glass of water and a tin of white tablets.

She smiled at him. "Thanks, honey," and used a little of what he'd brought, setting the rest on the table in front of her. "What's the picture?"

"Usual thing," he said, clearing his throat and settling beside her. His teeth worried his lip. "Want to see it?"

28

"Might as well," she answered. "Can't sleep." While she was watching horses, she knew he was looking at her thighs. "Another cowboy picture?"

"That's the style," he said, his eyes not galloping with the animals on the screen. They sat almost touching. His abdomen rose and sank. Before long he asked her, "How d' you feel now?"

"Can't tell yet," she told him, crossing a leg.

And he made his throat move. "Look," he said touching her ruffle, "you're taking chances sitting next to me in that thing." He sent his fingers along the edge of it, for a trace feeling indefinably smooth skin.

"Am I?" she asked, not calmly.

He nodded. "It's so soft," and touched her again.

She looked hard at the picture. "Want me to put on my coat?"

"No," he said, "uh-uh," and moved nearer until their bodies were touching lightly and took her hand and held it. And the horses went on without her. "Oh, Jeannie, Jeannie . . . Ohhh." Whispering—"Jeannie, babe," pressing his mouth on her loveline. It set her tingling and she touched his face. He kissed her throat, her mouth, felt her excitement. "You've got electricity in you, babe," he whispered. "I was going through something with you in there."

"So was I," she told him, and pressed her lips on his shoulder. Ignited, he lifted her onto his lap and his hands caressed under her robe. She felt his hard thighs through cloth, until he panted, "This's in the way." And she thrilled to the feel of air on her skin. His hot palms caressed her nipples, and then his mouth. Moist, warm, she held him without seeing. His hands sweated over her nudeness. Then, "Aw, wait a second," and he put her away from him while he was converting the couch into a bed, she stood craving for the bumping and scraping to end. And when it

29

did finally, he hurried out of the rest of his clothes, mad nearly, and lifted her up.

Now she was on a roomier softness, feeling his lips on her body. And holding each other they sank and rose so close now, her headache gone, he commanding, she yielding, at last whispering, "Yes, oh, yes, yes!"

Chapter Four

Early Monday morning Jean returned to Midwestern well-dressed and contrite. No one would see her. Humiliated for having tried, she walked alone past Jackson Park to the elevated and then trained downtown to a movie. The picture replayed nearly three times. And later, she didn't have to tell Ferris how things were. He knew. The way she walked and looked. She asked him, "What am I going to do?"

He said, "Stay here."

She didn't answer yes or no, but went to the kitchen where he said the paper was and turned to the want ads. She couldn't see the words. He came to the doorway and said, "Cuss, cry, anything."

She said, "I feel like someone threw me away."

"They did," he told her gently and walked over and put his hands on her shoulders. "Wait 'til tomorrow."

"And then what?" she wanted to know. "Things'll be better?"

He said, "No, they'll be just as bad, but you won't notice it so much." He massaged the back of her neck. "Babe, sweet, let me tell you something. This's a helluva life. And being black, you've got to be tougher. I mean inside. Don't let it break you down."

31

And before his strong hands left her, she knew she would stay.

She cashed in her bus ticket.

Before the end of the week the want ads came into focus, but nothing was in them. She hadn't any special skills, and anyway it was a poor time of year for anything that she was willing to do. She knew how some of those jobs were. The owners paid for groveling. And if you didn't grovel, you were in and out in a week. And while you were there, you caught hell from those who could, who wouldn't accept you no matter what. They'd each had fifteen minutes of education and resented any brown-skinned man or woman with any more. They ganged up on you, sneering you down to their size, and then despised you for shrinking. Besides, she wasn't thinking straight. All she could do was hate the rest of the world and wonder how she could work things out in the long run.

She called Bernie at Ferris' expense. He said Chris wasn't any better. And how was Jeannie? She lied, "Okay, Bernie." And he was to tell his mother, hello. Jean called him about once a week after that for about a month, and later about half as often. It was always the same.

Living with Ferris had its comforts, but still wasn't easy. He had quite a temper. And Jean knew with her own moodiness and hypersensitivity she was something of a problem. Anyhow, she saw that he came home to a clean, neat apartment. Sometimes the owner gave her flowers for the table, said he didn't mind having free extra tenants in his house as long as they weren't troublemakers. Ferris had a set of car keys made for her and taught her how to drive.

She got used to cooking whatever he liked. And once a week they went out riding or to a show. Or to get a better class of beer at one of the clubs. That usually happened on Fridays. On Saturdays, as a rule, he left her alone, going off to play poker, more often than not, losing. If he won, they ate steak. And he'd be more tender at night. They'd lie together in each other's arms, her softness, his strength joined and moving. It was never like that if he lost.

The first of the hot months came. And he came home in the middle of the week growling. She was settled in the kitchen going over the want ads, a fetish by then. And he nearly knocked over a stool sitting on it. His skin was a poor fit for his feelings. "What's wrong, honey?" she wanted to know. He poured it all out, several curses at a time. She translated as fast as she could. He'd been fired.

"But why?"

" 'Cause the foreman at the factory don't like black folks no kind a way. He's one a those white-assed bastards wants you to bow down so he can kick your butt. All the time needling me and pushing me. You know what I mean. That sneaky kind. Get you off to yourself and say something about your color. Or bring up some stupid thing he knew damn well you weren't going to stand for. And then he'd tell you to do something wrong and say he didn't. Get you in trouble. Make you look bad upstairs. And how're you going to know at the time? Just couldn't take anymore. That ain't my bag, babe."

"You mean—"

"I hit him. Damn right." He slammed his hands together knuckle to knuckle. "Yeah, I know what you'd say. I shoulda put out my hand and grinned, that's all right, ole buddy. That nonviolent stuff. The guy's a two-cent tyrant, babe. And tell you something from knowing bigger ones. I ain't never seen nonviolence win over a damn tyrant yet."

"What d'you want for supper?" she asked lamely, not willing to argue.

He mumbled he didn't care. "Anything."

He never wanted to be touched when he was like that. She knew what to expect that night. Total disregard or all-out war. She feared either. She said sympathetic things and for supper put a good meal before him. He splashed around in it with his fork until it was cold. Around eight o'clock he slammed out of the house. And it was late when he came back. She had stayed up unoccupied and pensive. He said he wanted to eat. He wasn't drunk and he wasn't sober. She fixed him something hot and he ate fast, numb to the taste, and left her the dirty dishes. When they were clean it was three in the morning. And she dragged herself to the bedroom, passing him in his usual place. He had his eyes closed, not sleeping, full of tension. She got ready for bed. For him if he wanted her. And seeing his crinkly crown, waited nude between the sheets.

Until she lost consciousness.

Sunrise was coloring the room when she woke up. He hadn't come to bed. And not seeing him, afraid, she hurried to the doorway.

He'd shifted to the other end of the couch, and hearing her, twisted around, saw her body. "Thought you'd gone out," she said.

Getting up slowly, he went to her. His hand touched her breast. She lowered her eyes. "Naw, I'm right here," he said, talking low. "Think I'll stay in today. Go see The Man first of the week." It was Friday. He settled his mouth on hers, felt her respond. From lying awake all night, his eyes were red. Stubble stood out on his chin. For a moment he held her, then traced her warm curves, whispering, "I want you, babe. I want you." And he kissed her again before they went into the bedroom.

Ferris found a job, not the following Monday but two weeks later. Factory work like the other. On payday they ate at one of

34

the newer restaurants lighting up Cottage Grove farther south. And he bought her perfume that she liked, and sheer lingerie that he liked. She could smile with him then and share an embrace. And each day they were together without the world braking and screeching.

It wasn't long before he lost that line of work. Because of another boss. And after he explained it, she guessed Ferris was right. Except that back in Des Graces she'd known a goodly number of men with bad bosses who had somehow managed to work steadily until retirement. But then maybe they had been wrong. Anyhow, she didn't argue about it. Just told him, "Don't worry, honey. We'll make out okay."

This lag outlasted the other. She learned it wasn't anything new. Ferris had job-hopped or had been hoofed out so many times before. He was always expecting something different from what he got or demanding this or that, she wasn't sure what. Though she guessed he was right in a way. He was quick and intelligent, trying to stand straight in a horizontal box. That was impossible, but just the same she didn't blame him. It was what she had against Des Graces—those boxes—and against Midwestern. And a man certainly had to try to stand even if he couldn't.

Ferris bivouaced in beer and let his face raise thicker stubble before using his razor. Jean dressed for more job interviews than she could count, and got none of them. He told her not to bother. That he'd take care of her. He liked her body and the feel of his apartment with her in it. Several times she mentioned marriage like some casual current event, as much as she wanted it. He said, "Nah," dropping his lower lip, nesting criticism in his eyebrows. "Not no more, baby. I had one time." He wasn't going through that again. "This way if you want to cut loose, ain't all that crap with a lawyer and callin' each other names in court." That didn't help her feel any better.

Fall came, flew old leaves like secondhand confetti. For weeks they'd been living on compensation. A friend of Ferris' told him about a company that was hiring. He looked into it and came home with an identification card. Jean was glad. It meant he wouldn't be surly, and arguing with her over nothing, criticizing her cooking, or anything, for that matter.

She called Bernie. He said her sister was coming along real good. His voice was cheerful. Jean could write to her now. 'Course she wasn't to feel bad if Chris didn't answer just yet. Jean understood.

Around October, one of the department stores downtown began calling for extra clerks for the holidays. And Jean made a pilgrimage to one of the biggest. She got the job and would be in accessories. Thrilled, she told Ferris. Glumly, he said that was nice. It was hard to know if he meant it. But anyhow, when she counted her forty-eight-hour-a-week dollars, she didn't care. She bought herself a box of candy, and some clothes, and foods she'd been craving. For Ferris she got several cartons of brew and a pair of house slippers. Over the weekend he coddled his feet and filled his middle.

With her bringing in money, they spent more. Sometimes, he borrowed from her. He never knew where his paycheck went, and she knew better than to ask. When Christmas came he didn't give her a present. Hurt, she kept it to herself. With a discount she picked out two shirts for him, put them in a fancy box, and wrapped them in pretty paper and ribbon. "Damn! Slipped my mind," he said. And he meant it. He had other things crowded inside him. "I'll pick up something later." He never did. And Jean, remembering, never brought it up.

The department store held on to a few of its temporary clerks. She was one of them. The work wasn't fun or stimulating, and it was hard on the arches and nerves. But anyway, it helped. Once in a while, Ferris would ask her for "a buck or two."

She'd say, "In my purse." Before very long he stopped asking.

Winter blew hard off the great frozen lake. And mornings of forced early rising stole the intensity out of Jean's color. In February Ferris was free again. This time he'd quit. He told her why, and she listened with dark circles under her eyes. There wouldn't be any compensation. Often after that she found money missing from her purse. He hadn't stolen it. Just took it by silent consent. When she hid it somewhere in the apartment, he found it. They argued about that. He couldn't locate a job and their debts were piling up. His spending pace hadn't changed. His beer mug was just as full as it had ever been. Knotted over the way his life was going, he cursed more and called her uncomplimentary names. In bed he fought her into paralysis, proud to have her and desperate, and afterward, guilty and drained.

A letter came from Chris. Things, it said, were back to normal. And when was Jean coming home? Chris and just everyone missed her. Back to normal. Jean danced around and cheered. That meant her sister was doing some serious thinking about how she'd landscape her garden and making pretties for the house, cooking the way only she could. Jean conjured up a glimpse of her. Little old Chris with that high voice of hers, always so eager to please. Well, she was going to save some money one way or another and go back at least for a weekend.

Spring came snowing meanly or spilling too much rain. Noisy wind berated Jean on the streets going to work or coming from it. With some of the customers she was jumpy and tense. And one day she stepped on the scale in the bathroom. She'd lost weight. Suddenly, it was all insane, Ferris forever calling her a bitch, and she feeling like one. She didn't want to sleep with him anymore. Wanted to run and run and run.

Suddenly, she was leaving him.

Ferris wore undershorts. There were metal cans on the floor. His fingers were laced across his belly, and he lay on the couch. "What?" he mumbled, scribbling trouble between his eyes.

"I said I'm leaving you."

He sat up in a hurry. "You crazy?"

"Think I have been," she sighed.

"Now wait a minute. What brought this on?"

She said, "Everything. I just can't take anymore, that's all."

He rubbed away an itch under his thigh. "Aw now, look, babe, let's talk about it, okay? I got enough troubles. Don't come in here with nothin' like this."

"It's not there anymore," she said stiffly.

He got up and tried to take her in his arms, "Babe, now listen—"

"No, don't, Ferris—don't." She squirmed away from him.

"What d' you think this is? You're just going to walk out of here, is that it?"

"I wanted to before this," she told him wearily. "But after all you did for me—I couldn't."

"You can now, huh?" He changed his accent, "Done got rich wicha damn job—" and changed again—"Aw, Jeannie, honey—okay, so I'm not up too high. I'm down, baby, I know it—but wait."

"For what?" she asked him. "So you can get another job and lose it? I've got to get somewhere. I can't stand still and take this. Being what you want me to be, not knowing who I am half the time."

Ferris clapped a spread palm on his hair, paced, scowled. She could smell his sweat. "Dammit, I don't want you to go. I'm not going to let you."

She was afraid of him. "Please, Ferris, let me alone. I'm going to get my things." Most of her money was pinned in her brassiere. The rest was in her purse. Going to the bedroom, she took it from the top of the bureau, opened it, and took something out of it.

And Ferris snatched the purse out of her hands. "No!" he said. The shock of that made her stop. And then he softened, asking, "Want me to tell you I love you, is that it? Okay, I love you." His throat wasn't clear.

"You never said it before. Don't say it now," she told him bitterly. "I'm going to pack my things."

"I said no."

"Ferris please—"

"No now. Sit down and let's talk this thing out."

"I don't want to talk anymore," she said. "It won't do any good. The way things are, I hate myself—"

"And me too, huh?"

She didn't answer that, said, "I'm getting my things. Give me my purse,"

"And me too?" He growled, keeping the purse. He blocked her way. Trying to get past him, she couldn't. "Baby, you ain't taking one thing outa here," he said, "not your books, not your clothes—"

And so she gave in. "All right. Okay, Ferris." She wilted. She knew he would hold her and, not meaning to, maybe hurt her. Because of the way things were. And she didn't want to be hurt.

He relaxed, grinning. "Come on over here." He nodded his head toward the sofa.

"In a minute," she promised. "I've got to go to the toilet first." She went into the bathroom and slipped the bolt in quietly while he sat down and put her handbag on a cushion. He paid no attention to the door being locked. Or maybe he didn't hear it.

He was puffed up on twenty proof and a kind of success. And success was what he needed in the worst way.

She was in the bathroom too long. He called her name. Could be crying, he thought. He called out again. Got up and went to the bathroom door. "Jeannie? . . . Hey, Jeannie." The truth thumped him. There was no one in there. He tried to force the handle. It wouldn't work. He fought with a foot—one blow—and shattered wood along the hinges. Inside the toilet paper was blowing gently. Hanging next to the wall where the window had been open all day. He looked out at the porch roof below and remembered the drainpipe. Far behind in the race, he rushed to the bedroom closet and yanked down a pair of pants. Stooping, angry, he jerked them on and ran out the back door and down the stairs. A latch was holding the door below. He attacked it and quickly invited darkness creamed with moonlight and sending up the so-long hum of his car. It came to him then what Jean had taken out of her purse. The car keys. Sure. All the time she'd been planning. Getting the jump on him. "It's in my name, dammit!" he yelled, running over flowers to the fence, yelling down the alley, "You ain't gonna get away with that! I'll have the cops on your ass!"

Chapter Five

Jean had waited for several minutes before sliding down the drainpipe. The dress she was wearing wasn't designed for the trip. She hurt her knee. It was only a scratch. But falling gave her a jolt. Afraid someone would hear her, worse, that Ferris would, she crossed the yard in a crouch and went toward the alley beyond. His car was in its accustomed place behind the red stained boards protecting chrysanthemums. She climbed because the gate would have squeaked, telling her arms and legs, "Hurry."

Ferris Boone got his car back. The police found it that night two blocks from where he lived, near a city bus stop.

Jean asked for a change to another department at the store where she worked, and moved from the first floor to household appliances seven floors above. She had spent the night cowering in a cheap hotel. By the time she'd found a room somewhere else, Ferris found her waiting on a customer, smiling, not happily but easily for the first time in months. When she saw him she lost her composure and forgot all about the woman who wanted a mixer. He didn't seem to be anyone to fear, except that he was there. "I want to talk to you. When you're through," he told her, keeping his voice low and even.

Disconcerted, she said, "I'd rather not." But anyhow, he wouldn't go away. She made the sale. The lady charged it and left them together.

He whispered, "I need you. I'm going crazy. That wasn't no way to act. Taking my car. And me sitting there thinking you're coming out."

She told him, "Let me alone," that he was never to come there again. He pleaded with her. Her mind was made up, riding her midheels to another counter. He followed. No, he wasn't going to let her alone. He'd be back. Any day in the week. Because he needed her. No woman ever got to him like she did. And if she wanted her things they were there for her. She said he was deranged. He said, if he was, she made him that way. He left her with that.

Three days later he came back, and at first he wasn't loud. And then he was terrible. Something he said sounded like a threat. Jean's customer gasped, "What in the world!"

The floor manager, a look-alike for Napoleon, came over and asked if anything was wrong. Nearly distracted, Jean told him, "No," that it would be all right. It wasn't. A crowd gathered. And she ran to the employees' room, crying shamefully.

Ferris didn't know why he did what he did. When he left the last time, he had no such thing in mind. It just kept building and building. The day before, he had to borrow some cash. And one company was clawing for payments or the return of his car. High on hurt and low on pride just then, he stayed up most of the night going over the reasons he'd been fired or had quit. They still seemed to him like good ones. Every place he'd ever worked was making something for progress. And yet they wanted him to think and act like his granddaddy. He couldn't. Why he hadn't finished high school and gone to college, reaching his own mental timberline and being above some of the muck, was something he asked himself time and again in the half dark with a can of beer in his grip. Answering, Because it wasn't easy. High-salaried folks who planned other folks' lives said it was. But then they had plans for world peace too and for feeding all the poor.

The seventh-floor manager was fairly well liked by his clerks. He hadn't been known to play favorites by color or ever make the day long for anyone. So when he sent a woman after Jean it was because of the pressures of the busiest hour. Customers were waiting. The department was short-handed. Fearing Ferris, Jean refused to come out. The manager sent another verbal message that the woman toughened a bit. And Jean yelled through her tears that she was staying where she was.

Before the store closed, she got a notice that she no longer worked there.

He should have understood, she thought, hating the manager and everybody who looked like him. She went to the rooming house where she lived, wondering when the horror was going to stop. She couldn't go up for going down. Too jangled for sleep she wasted a night and got up early, stalking the morning paper. There was a note in her mailbox without an envelope, quickly scrawled. It read, "Know where you live now, Jeannie. Followed you home last night. I'll be back. Even if you move."

She crushed the harassment and, frightened, went into the building again. In her room she raced through decisions. She couldn't stay there any longer. Without a job, getting another place to live was next to impossible. And one thing was certain. Chicago had the black flag up for her. She was getting out. As fast as she could. Chris and Bernie wanted to see her. Okay. It would mean housework for a little while. And then what? Des Graces forever? Hardly. The West Coast. Why not? Somewhere far away. From Ferris, from a bad start. Start over. She'd heard many times San Francisco was quite a city. Well, she'd have time to think about that. In Des Graces. "Good old, wonderful old, heavenly old Des Graces," she said.

A pay telephone was in the hall of her building. She had some change in her purse, more than enough for the night rate. Leaving her room, she called Des Graces, and Chris came through. It was wonderful hearing Jean's voice. How was she? Jean lied, "Just fine. I'd like to come home, and was hoping to stay with you and Bernie for a while." The pause was short. Of course she could. What did she think? And hurry. She could have the upstairs back room.

"I was thinking about tomorrow."

Another pause. Then, "Oh, that's grand. We'll be looking for you." They long-distanced love to each other.

Jean had bought one small overnight bag big enough for her few replacements of clothes left behind. Ferris, she supposed, had thrown them away with her books. Some of her other things were at Chris and Bernie's, taken from the old home after her mother died. Casual wear, levis, T-shirts, old shoes, and so forth. After packing, she told the owner she'd be moving. Used to defectors, he took it in stride. Besides, it wouldn't be any trouble renting the room. And he was ahead in the rent.

Starting the ride downtown on a train high up, Jean got off underground at State and Randolph. She had seventy dollars and twenty cents.

The trip was long and slow. And since it was Thursday not many people were traveling. She had a double seat to herself. She was glad of that. On the way there were countless stops. She stayed on board, thinking about her sister. Beautiful bubbly Chris. How good it would be seeing her again! And how long it had been!

When the driver called out, "Des Graces," she retrieved her bag from the overhead rack and got off in the clear afternoon light. A few people were scattered on the loading zone, passengers and the launchers. She passed some of them, walking slowly through the depot to the street. She looked around, feeling the newness of that time in her life coupled with the same old evidence. "Exactly the same," she sighed, affronted that it was. Across the street from her was a small health food store, and she thought, "What's health anyway? Eat their stuff and I won't hurt anymore? I'm free suddenly? . . . Maybe they have got the answer. At those prices I can't afford to find out."

Not far from where she stood, a taxi idled at the curb. Hiring it, she rode for several miles to the third cottage on a peaceful street. Except that some of the paint was peeling. And the grass had more weeds than anything else. That wasn't the way it had been before. She gave the driver, a close-mouthed man, the sixty-five-cent fare and a ten-cent tip, and he went on to other business. Willow trees stood every twenty feet, tall old ones, She walked under the nearest, liking its shade since it was a hot day. Some of the neighbors were sitting on their porches on the wicker furniture that had long been the style in that block, older folks, a few young wives. Jean waved to those she knew would wave back. They told her how good she looked, and to be sure and come see them. Aimless talk to a prodigal, or most of it anyway. And she guessed they wanted to hear about the school riot firsthand, old as the news was by then. Again she observed the condition of the property where her sister and brother-in-law lived, then went up the path to the stoop and rang the bell. Instantly it came to her what was strange about the house besides its appearance. All the windows were closed and it was locked up. In July that was never done. Was anyone home? Fearful, she started to look in a window when a face filled the one in front of her. Bernie's. His thin friendly mouth, small thin nose, kind gray eyes. At first he was half-hidden by a dingy curtain. Quickly he opened the door. "Hiii, little sister," he said, making himself sound cheerful and showing a great deal of strain. His shirt and trousers looked tacky. Away from work, they never had before. Lines trailed down from his nose to his mouth. His long concave face was thinner. And something recent and unpleasant stained his eyes.

She answered, "Hi, Bernie, how are you?" It was so good seeing him. "Where's Chris?"

"Upstairs," he told her, unlocking the screen. "Be right down soon's she gets herself together." He shoved back the barrier, took Jean's bag from her, kissing her fraternally on the cheek, and let her go past him into the hall. There wasn't any sunshine in it. Most of the shades beyond it were down, and not to keep the house cool. There was air-conditioning. Knowing what she had on her mind, he said, "Kind of dark in here, huh? Well, make yourself at home." The hall was drab and dusty. And an empty bowl on a narrow table near one wall that always held summer flowers had a long crack down the side of it where the pieces had been glued together.

She felt uneasy about the house, about the way her brother-in-law was acting, when walking sounded upstairs. She lifted her eyes to it, feeling better. Chris was coming. Bernie, who had been holding her bag with a thought of taking it up to her room, changed his mind and set it down beside the last step. "No rush," he said and, "Look, got something to get out of the basement. I was fixing it so you could use it tonight. Be right back."

"Okay, Bernie," Jean said, still watching the sound. She saw her sister's feet, the old flat sandals, then saw her.

Chris was fat. Her slacks and blouse were faded, a little soiled, and her hair was swept up sloppily. Dark rings were under her eyes. Her color was poor. And she wasn't pretty. "Jeannie!" She cried, inventing effervescence.

More happy than shocked, Jean sent out her arms and they hugged each other.

When they parted, Chris said, "Don't look at me. I'm a mess, girl. I've put on so much weight."

"Oh, you'll get rid of it," Jean told her, "and be your old self again."

Chris changed, looking terribly worried. "Am I that bad? Tell me the truth now."

Jean saw that she couldn't. "No, of course not. Just different." She said it so well, her sister relaxed. "Bernie doesn't like me this size. Doesn't say much but I can tell." And Jean recognized some of the same stain in Chris's eyes that she'd seen before in his. Leading the way to the kitchen, Chris said, "Know you're hungry. Haven't eaten, have you?"

"Uh-uh." Jean was following. She wondered if Chris knew about the riot. She suspected not. The mouthy neighbors probably had stopped talking about it by the time Chris had left the hospital.

"Don't pay any attention to the house," the shorter woman said, "I've been so busy."

"I won't. You know me," Jean answered, thinking, busy with what? The kitchen was barbarous, a catch-all for old newspapers and rags and magazines and dishes, some dirty, some cracked, that were strewn over cabinets, tables, and chairs. Rather than raise the shades, Chris turned on a light. Dirty curtains kept their places still, and smears were on the door. The floor hadn't been mopped in ages and only carelessly swept. "How's the garden doing?" Jean wanted to know.

Getting things to eat out of the refrigerator, Chris said that she hadn't planted one this year. She'd always done it, but hadn't felt

47

well enough. She sliced ham and the knife clattered against the plate. Had she been ailing a lot? She said, "Nothing serious. Feel fine now." Pouring iced tea, she spilled some and snatched a napkin from a box on the table and wiped it up. The table didn't get cleared in a rush. By the time it was dressed in its dull cloth and wearing plates and cutlery, Bernie rose up from the basement with a small lamp in his right hand and ascended to the second floor. He smiled only, going by, his mind fixed on getting rid of what he was holding and washing up and on something besides. Jean had aways felt at ease with him. But now she didn't.

When he came down again, he didn't return to the kitchen right away, but went into the living room and read the paper. Before long, Chris called out to him that supper was ready, and he joined her and Jean, and sat at the head of the table. They all served themselves, Jean first. She chewed slowly, hardly tasting anything and saying how delicious everything was. That made her sister smile. Bernie ate fast, filling his long hollow jaws like a man looking for love in his plate. "Going to stay here and get a job huh, little sister?" He said finally.

"For a while at least. Until I get enough money."

"And then what? Back to Chicago?" Chris was listening only, making her fork move too many times in her food.

"No, got San Francisco on my mind."

"Going to be a hippie?" Chris smiled.

Jean giggled, "Very funny."

Bernie's eyebrows arched. "S.F., yeah? How 'bout that? Hear it's pretty nice out there. But I don't know, you count it all up, deals the same for *us* all over."

"Besides, they mark all the cards," Chris put in.

"And that's not the point anyway," Jean came out. "I'm sick of the same old game. The way it's played I lose no matter who deals, marked cards or no. But just the same I'll try my luck out there."

He asked, "When're you going?"

"Around the first of September. That ought to be a good time for finding work."

"Kind of like to travel myself," Bernie said as if he never would.

"Well, maybe both of you can come out and see me when I get settled," Jean told him.

He chewed, "Maybe . . . I meant to tell you, you're looking good, girl. Lost some weight, didn't you?"

"Too much," she answered.

"Just the same," he said, "it looks good. Not the same skinny kid I used to know."

Jean laughed. "Haven't been for a long time." Seeing Chris was irritated, she got on another subject. "How's the fishing? Still catching the big ones?"

He shrugged. "The fish're getting too smart for me. But I'm going tomorrow. Same old place, same old tackle."

"Like always," Chris came in. "Ever see a Saturday between April and October when he didn't?" She sounded unnecessarily critical, trying to make it sound like humor.

Bernie lowered his head, which was already too close to his plate. His shoulders were bent over and his neck set in deep, and drab short sleeves freed most of his sinewy arms. "Got to take Chris to the doctor's first," he said. And when Jean looked worried, "Just a regular checkup. He's a nice bird, but sometimes he takes all day."

"I've been feeling much better, though," Chris said.

Afterward, Jean helped with the dishes. That done, they all went into the living room, a messy place hiding in the dark. Chris preferred a lamp to opening blinds. They talked about what had happened in Des Graces during the last year. Nothing had happened. It was still foundering in corn, and captaining in paternalistic clichés, and getting I-know-my-place answers, still giving colored folks kernels for money.

"And how was Chicago?"

Jean couldn't think of anything good to say about it. Chris asked how school was.

"So-so."

"I heard about the riots. That was all the talk at the hospital."

"I—I'm transferring my credits," Jean lied, rattled by Chris's knowing, "to a college on the coast."

"Hope you don't lose any," said Bernie. "What'd you do all last year? After that mess, I mean." His reaction to Jean's lie didn't discolor his behavior.

"Worked. At a department store. They just laid me off the other day. Too much help and not enough work. Newcomers like me had to go."

"I was saying to myself, my sister's in that mess with all the white folks," Chris doubled back. "Course, I remember how you used to stick in with them when you were in high school."

"What d'you mean?" Jean asked. "Most of my friends were colored."

"Yes, but you know yourself you were the only one of *us* taking up with them at all."

"Well, now I hate them." Jean grimaced. "After what the cops did to me, and that ratty chancellor and the dean."

"What about the students?" Bernie wanted to know.

"Oh, some of them were okay," said Jean. "That short-termy-I'm-with-you-to-the-end type." Bernie laughed at that a little, and it sounded good to Jean.

Except for that, she felt like a stranger. Because of the contention between her sister and brother-in-law, and feeling the scattershot of it. Things were out of joint, unreal. And yet it was real, just as Chicago had been. Just as if trouble had trailed her here. Or maybe this was the full circle of it. What a sickening notion. They watched television together because it saved questioning and answering. Is that what was going on all over? Jean asked herself. There was too much that shouldn't or couldn't be talked about, so people kept their eyes and ears on the fakery? Coast to coast?

And Ferris, was that what he was doing? Or was he out somewhere drinking? Or trying to kick the building down where she used to live, or just riding around? Oh, to hell with Ferris.

They stayed up late, seeing the last screen credit. Jean was all out of energy by then and, counting her output the last two days, she needed, she decided, to sleep forever. "Think I'll go to bed," she said unclearly.

"All of us," yawned Bernie rising from a chair.

"What time're you going fishing?" Jean asked.

"Not too early. Take Chris 'round quarter to nine, hit the road after that. Told Jay and Felix" (Jean knew them) "I'd meet them out there. They're leaving 'bout seven or so."

"You won't get much sleep that way," she told him.

"Don't need much," he answered going over to the stairs and picking up her bag. His hand found the stair and hall light while Chris put out the one in the living room. And in a higher place they all said goodnight. Jean's bag was set down just inside the door. Bernie had flicked the switch. The room was bright. And it was pretty. It had been polished and cleaned. Clean curtains hung at the windows and a pale green spread covered where she'd be sleeping. Chris, she guessed, must have worked all morning. Jean lowered the shades. They showed soil. It didn't matter. She sighed out of her clothes and took out her nighties. "When I get up I'll wash," she promised the pile on the floor. Dousing the light she went to the window nearest the bed, seeking air, with her mind on the way things were. And on Ferris who was probably sleeping with his head back against the couch and his legs thrust out, her slippers on his feet. Or maybe he wouldn't wear them as a sort of protest. Maybe he'd throw them away. She raised the shade, then the window, saw the stars like a shower of salt. From that angle there wasn't any moon. Across the yard a window darkened.

A knock woke Jean up. Another made her turn her head toward the door. "Jeannie." Bernie's voice.

"Yes?"

"Can I come in?"

"Uh-huh." Surprised. A clock on the nightstand had ticked past nine-fifteen. She pulled the sheet up as high as her chin.

He was wearing his fishing clothes, khaki trousers and jacket, a visor cap the same color, and sneakers. "Hi," he said, "did I wake you?"

"Doesn't matter. Is this clock right?"

"A little slow," he told her.

"I didn't even dream," she exhaled noisily. "Where's Chris?"

"Took her to the doctor's."

"Thought you were going fishing?"

"I am, in a few minutes." Shifting from one foot to the other, he put his hands in his pockets, saying, "Got to talk to you. That's why I came back. I couldn't say anything in front of Chris. The way she is."

"What d'you mean?" Jean asked him.

One of his hands came out for a second and moved around. "Aw—look, Jeannie, I love your sister. We've been together what is it? Eleven years. But things aren't right. You see how the house is."

"I noticed when I came in yesterday," Jean admitted, easier with him now.

He flopped into an overstuffed chair that was close to the door. "Jeannie, if something doesn't get straight soon, I'm going crazy." His forehead worked, rumpling his angular brows. "You see how she looks."

Jean nodded. "Like somebody else. I was shocked."

"That's the way I stay," Bernie let out. "I can't touch her. And then she's got this thing about me running around with other women. Dammit, if she doesn't let me near her, I'm going to have to. I'm a man. I can't keep this up. Sitting on the ground with a couple of hardheads, talking to some damn fish. You know yesterday when you came?" They'd been arguing. About something Chris imagined and blew up out of proportion, he said. She thought the neighbors were peeking in, so she insisted upon keeping the shades down, and the doors and windows closed. He wanted them up and open. "And she gave me hell." Just before Jean came.

"Seems like I walked in on a real to-do," Jean whispered hoisting her knees to a chest-high hill.

"And the house needs painting," Bernie went on, "and she won't let me do anything about it. Gets loud whenever I bring it up. Says we need that little bit of money. Okay, so we've spent a lot this last year on doctor's bills and all. But have you ever heard such a thing?"

"It's usually the other way around," and Jean smiled wanly. "Do you think she'll get well?"

He pressed one fist against his palm between his knees, which were spread apart and bent. "Aw, God help us if she doesn't. Throwing dishes. Broke that lamp I fixed yesterday." Jean saw it near her on the stand. "Doc says he sees a good deal of improvement. Sure be glad when I see it." He got up and paced.

53

"Maybe I shouldn't have come just now," Jean considered.

"Oh, don't think that," he told her. "She's glad you got here and so'm I. I just hope you can take it. Maybe you can help her get herself together. I'm stuck." He sat on the edge of the bed with his head down, looking helpless.

Jean felt sorry for him. "Guess we have to be patient," she murmured. "And maybe I can help some with the house."

"You know I'm glad I came back," he said, grinning, "and had a chance to talk to you. You can't go around letting it out any old place. Not in this town."

"I know," she said.

"And another thing that's bugging me," loose now, he went on and on, telling her about his wife's fantasies. And Jean listened sympathizing and feeling terrible that things were that way.

Neither of them heard the front screen door open downstairs or heard, following that, any unusual noise. Until, "What's this?" came from the hall. Chris was back.

Bernie shot up from the bed and turned around, looking, his wife was sure, guilty. She joined him and her sister quickly, wild in the eyes. "Uh-huh, uh-huh. That's the way you do me. Get me out of the house. Jean's looking so good. Thought I wouldn't notice. Little dumb Chris. Broke your neck getting back here—"

"Now come on, honey," Bernie frowned, "don't start that stuff."

"What stuff? Think I can't see? The way you got this room all cleaned up for her." Here I thought she did it, Jean told herself. "What'd I do, come back too soon for you?" Chris eyed Jean still beneath the sheet but with her knees down now.

"Cut out that noise," Bernie demanded, going to the open window and closing it.

"I'll make as much noise as I want to. Thought I wouldn't catch you. My own sister."

Jean said, "Nothing's happened."

"And nothing's going to," he said, trying to be calm.

"Not if I have anything to do with it," Chris sneered.

Bernie went over to her and tried to put his arm around her. She slashed him away with her arm, shouting, "Let me alone!" And shouting at Jean, "You damn slut, get out of that bed! Get out of my house! You hear? Go on to California or get a job or whatever. But get the hell out of here!"

Jean sank inside. Bernie said, "Now hold it, Jeannie, just don't pay any attention. She doesn't mean it."

"Don't I?" Chris shouted again. "I said get out of my house!" A frenzy was coming and both Jean and Bernie knew it. Chris thought she hated her sister, and it was the same as if she did.

Either way, Jean didn't care. Her already fragmenting hope was torn apart. Des Graces had no rooming houses. The hotels were too expensive. And all of a sudden she wanted to get away as quickly as she could. The cheapest way to the west she could think of just then was the bus. "Let me get dressed," she rasped, staring at the clothes on the floor. They wouldn't get washed in Des Graces. "Where're my old clothes? The things you took from the other house."

"Look in this closet and that bureau," Chris said, flinging her hand twice. Then she and her husband went out, closing the door and taking their distress downstairs. Jean got up in sections, and put on her robe.

She didn't stay long in the bathroom. The clothes she put on were rough and plain. It didn't take her long to pack. She left the bed unmade, followed the dim hall to the stairs, and went down.

The other two were in the living room with a rug's width between them, not talking, though Bernie had tried. Jean said one thing before saying good-bye. "You're wrong, Chris, and maybe someday you'll know you are. I hope so."

"You're not leaving town?" Bernie asked.

She said, "Yes."

"Not San Francisco?" She nodded. "But what about a job here?"

"Think I'd better go now. I don't think the other would work out anyway."

"What about money?"

"Got enough," Jean lied.

"Now wait, ju-just wait," he begged.

"No," Jean said going to the door. And then she said the last words and left the two of them.

She'd passed three other houses when Bernie came out running. "I told you it was bad," he said, "but I didn't think it was like that. Don't go."

She said, "I have to. I know I can't stay here." And after he tried to change her mind, he offered to drive her to the depot. She shook her head. "No, I'll take the bus."

"You're not mad at me, too?"

"Course not. But the condition she's in, she wouldn't understand if you did that."

"Guess not," he agreed.

"Let's hope she pulls out of it," Jean told him, then told herself, and that I do.

"Good luck, sweetie," he sighed and touched her shoulder. "Take care, hear? And when you get there, write. Let us know and—"

"Yes?" Jean waited.

"Don't hold it against her." The girl looked away from him. He looked at the clothes she was wearing, frowning at how they changed her, but not saying anything about them.

She said something final, not harshly, and went away before he did, walking two blocks to the transit stop. Not much later, she

56

was in front of the interstate bus depot, whispering painfully, "In Des Graces one day, right out the next." Mentally, she counted her money. She had fifty-nine dollars and sixty-five cents.

Inside the depot, she found out how much the trip would cost. Fifty-three, fifty. So she could think better, she went over to a bench near one wall, and sat down. The ticket, deducted from what she had, left six dollars and fifteen cents. She'd have to eat en route. That would take a dollar or two at least. If God got her a job right away, it would be easy to get a loan until payday. Only, she wasn't going to bet on that.

She was scared. What should she do? Take a chance anyhow? She knew another way. And that scared her even more.

She could hitchhike.

Well, why not? Jeannie, look, if things get too tough, say about half way, hop on a bus. Even that much'd be a saving. She went back to the ticket window and asked about the fare from Denver and from Salt Lake City to San Francisco, and learned that either would take more than half her cash.

But hitchhiking . . . She *had* to get out of Des Graces. Go somewhere different. And maybe then she could pull herself together. She decided she'd better buy a traveler's check at the bank in the next block. Could be risky carrying too much money.

All the way to the First National, she kept hoping for a miracle. Like a lifetime full of twenty-dollar bills lying on the sidewalk.

There was a man at the first teller's window. And she bought a fifty-dollar check from him for fifty dollars and fifty cents. For some reason, she felt much poorer. And walking to the transit stop, her body felt numb.

The westbound city bus came quickly, and she climbed on board along with a handful of other people, and gave her fare to the railly, indifferent driver. She sat in front thinking, there won't be any miracles. Her clothes, she guessed, were the best for the trip. T-shirt, levis, a lightweight jacket, socks and sneakers. A scarf covered her pigtail.

The bus was uncomfortable. It rattled, and not much later, screeched stopping. The door opened, she got off and hiked a little distance, then stared at corn and sky. At cars racing east and west. Her body came back to life, and it was a painful feeling. Setting her bag on sod, weeping nearly, she smiled and spread her feet apart, saying, "Here we go, Jeannie babe," and put her thumb out.

Chapter Six

When she was at Midwestern, some of the other girls used to hitchhike, taking short trips mostly, downstate or over to Indiana. She'd thought they were crazy.

"But this's really crazy," she said without moving her mouth. "Jeannie, what're you doing out here, standing like a fool? And the way you look—these crummy clothes. Okay, who's first? Let's put on the brakes, boys. Get your girl hitchhiker here . . . Come on, *somebody,* please." She didn't really feel like joking. But anyhow, it helped her keep the hatred out of her pose, and kept her bitterness from showing.

A farmer in a pickup truck took her a little way and showed her the best place to stand, a shady spot.

And three rides later she'd gone forty miles to a part of Iowa with scrubby weeds on both sides of the flat gray road. Cows grazed near where she stood for over an hour. Just as she was starting to droop, a small red truck pulled over. The driver was a lady who was plump and gray-haired and friendly. She drove Jean twenty miles, telling about her grandchildren. And the place where she left her wasn't bleak at all. There were maples, white houses with a good bit of space between, and flowers growing in their gardens. Swallows were in the air. They were singing. Jean looked up. And all around.

An old man came along in a Model T Ford. It moved pretty well. His clothes were neat and out of style, and he was only going ten miles. He said he was eighty-two, and had an Adam's apple jollying his goosey throat, and his air, if arthritic, was jaunty. He spent the time talking, asking Jean questions about her hiking and giving her a little advice. "Get a map from this gas station where I turn off up here. So you'll know where y'are if any of these birds you meet start leaving the highway for what they call a shortcut." And he said not to tell 'em where she's headin' 'til she found out where they were headin'. She thanked him for all that. And when he stopped, he put his hand on her knee. "Wouldn't be interested in a little sport, would you?"

Jean snapped, "No," and pushed his hand away, and climbed out of his car. Cocky about the effect he had caused, with the rest of his wick he put a toe on the gas, and the old chassis struggled north.

The station the old man had mentioned was also a general store, and quaint. Its owner was an older lady, placid, still pretty. She let Jean clean up in the washroom and gave her iced tea, "just for the company." Jean bought bread, processed cheese, and some fruit, and they sat and talked for a while. Before Jean left she asked for a map of the country. When the lady learned how far Jean was going, she dug out one for Iowa and for all the states beyond. Jean went back to the highway, thinking how nice the lady was, how easy to talk to. And how much she hated her. She didn't have to be that nice. Go out of her way. That's the way they are—hypocrites. Doing little favors for you, catching you off guard. And when you start feeling like a human being—

bam! Maybe she was nice. Probably. But anyhow Jean hated her. For one reason. Because if she made any exceptions, she'd start getting careless, trust the wrong person, get hurt again. And she didn't want that to happen.

She rode with a very nice man. And after that with a mother and daughter. Not much farther along she sat on a rock and made a sandwich. A tall man was walking east on her side of the highway as though walking were all he had. He asked her, "Got any money?" Like he was asking for the time.

She said no. He studied her clothes and the dust on them, took a contemptuous step, stopped, looked again, walked on.

A state trooper's car made a U-turn and came over to where she was. The trooper got out. Jean thought he was going to arrest her. She was scared. He asked her where she was headed and if she had any identification. She pulled out her wallet and showed him who she was, and then lied that she'd lost her bus fare. He was polite. He got back into his car and sped away. She relaxed. Later, other troopers would pass her in their cars without paying her any notice. She'd guess that word had been sent out to let her alone.

A fat white truck came to a halt. The letters on its side read, ICE CREAM. The driver bounced out, wiped his chins, and said, "Whew, hot day, ha ha." Jean agreed that it was. And then he opened a side door and reached into his truck, bringing out frozen bars, one vanilla and one chocolate. The chocolate he gave to Jean. She thanked him, thinking, brown for me, white for him, and bit hers. It was good. The man took three quick chomps and threw away a naked stick, while she went on licking and nibbling. When she finished, he asked her for a kiss.

She told him, "No."

"Okay," he grinned, and got back into his truck and bobbled off.

"Good grief," Jean said out loud, "no line, no feeling—no moving, no talking, no laughing, red light."

A salesman invited her into his car, a long, lovely, air-conditioned sedan. Fortyish, he was nice-looking, of medium build, wearing well-tailored clothes. And after they had been riding together for a while, he grew apprehensive, said, "I shouldn't have picked you up. I mean if we have an accident and they find you with me, what're people liable to think?"

"Hadn't thought about it," she told him, in spite of the air-conditioning, not feeling comfortable.

He muttered, "No, you wouldn't. But I'm the one who should worry. I've got a wife and two kids. I'm respected. If we have a crash and they found us—"

"Well, I hope we don't."

"I'm just saying . . . I was only doing you a favor. And it could turn into something ugly. At least that's what people who know me would think . . . the way it would be in all the papers."

"I'm sure it could be explained."

"You say." He showed more agitation. "We could get killed together. And then what? Who'd know for sure? . . . It's risky . . . I've got too much at stake . . . My wife—I'm letting you out at the next crossroad."

That was six miles from the ice cream truck. Depressed, Jean stared after the very fine car. Most of all, she missed the air conditioning.

The next man said he was wealthy. He was well dressed, close to fifty with quietly graying hair. Good-looking. Taller than Jean.

He told her, "I'm not interested in you. Let's make that clear. But I certainly think it's all right for a white man to have as much sex with a colored woman as he likes."

Jean dodged, "Do you travel much in your business?"

"The more the merrier."

"Haven't been too many places myself."

"I'm not saying this to give you any ideas. You don't mean a thing to me."

"They have more corn in this state than all the Midwest put together."

"Got a son at Yale. And if he wanted sex with one of you, fine. Just so there's no wedding."

"Folks say most of it's horse corn," Jean groaned, losing ground.

"No, don't marry any of them. It's different with a white man's daughter."

"Different how?" She gave up.

He looked at her, amazed. "Why, the name. You wouldn't want them to have our names."

Another salesman, short, stubby, and in his mid-fifties, said he knew all about *her* people. And what did Jean know about Roebuck?

"Nothing."

"Roebuck," he told her smugly, "started the business they call Sears." Jean heard only Negro history for forty miles.

High overhead a bird went by. After that ride had ended. "I wish I were you," she said, disgusted, and taking out her Iowa map and a pencil slashed a dark line from Des Graces to where she was. She was still too far from Nebraska. The sun had rolled ahead of her. Before long it would be night. And night out there wasn't for novices.

The Kansas man came up in his car, Caucasian like all the others though nearly as dark as she. He was handsome, not more than thirty-five. And he said he was going west for thirty miles. Said he was rich, except his car didn't show it. After ten slow-poke minutes he mentioned needing gas, and turned onto a side road. The station was supposed to be only a quarter of a mile from the highway. But when he kept going and going and the view got thicker and wilder, Jean ordered, "Take me back!" With fire in her eyes.

"Wait a minute," he complained, upset. "You're not afraid of me, are you? I'm not that kind of a fella. Just thought if you wanted to. I don't take advantage of any woman. Are you afraid of me? 'Cause if y'are I'm going to let you out right here." Miles from U.S. 30. "Tell me." He looked hurt. Jean said she wasn't. Her face lost its excitement and so did her voice. She believed he was a gentleman all along. Knew she didn't have to worry. "You mean that?" His eyes were slits and he was sweating. She told him, she did. That's why she was surprised when he turned off without giving her any choice. She wanted to make Omaha before it got dark. This slowed her down. He promised he'd take her back. "But anyway I thought you were afraid of me. I wouldn't. I'm no beast. Never have been. I'm a respectable farmer with a wife and four children." By then he wasn't so upset. "And I want you to respect me. Do you?" She said that she did. "Then I'll take you back." Going over old ground they were both quiet.

On the highway again, he wanted to shake hands with her. She went along with that. And seconds later, while his car was hurrying away, her knees buckled.

The out-of-the-way tour had stolen daylight. "I need a long ride," she said, and frowned hard. "Across the Missouri. Not a two-step to the next bush." Struggling, she made up a smile.

A boy saw it from an old topless car. He was small and sallow, at most nineteen. And his coarse gray clothes were wrinkled. "Going fourteen mile," he told her sounding like a Southerner. Jean didn't want to get in with him, but did anyway. Off and on he glanced at her and that was all. When he stopped, letting her climb free, the sun had gone and it was twilight.

He creaked west. And she said to herself, "You never know." He'd looked like the worst mistake she could have made. Feeling easier, she put up her thumb.

Traffic rumbled in concert going east. Her side was lonely. Finally, a car came.

The same car.

The teenager whined, "Want t' show y' somethin'." Opening his pants in front, he pulled out his penis, a little limp thing, saying, "Y' want some?"

"*Leave me alone!*" Jean screamed. "*Get out of here!*" He shrank and hid his organ, then scrambled off down the road.

And shaken, because of the day, the whole year, she begged for Omaha. For a long time. Standing in the dark.

She forced herself to calm down, and hoped her light jacket would show up enough. She didn't want to get hit by a car or a truck. It was chilly now. Her fit had drained her and she felt the weather more. The land looked mean in the dark. Her shoulder ached. Her lower arm was tired. Clouds hid the stars and moon. Ten-ton trucks showed up all at once, roaring the other way. During the day most of the mass had been autos, but now the route belonged to the big beasts, diesels huffing smoke, long silver trailers whose headlights found her, lost her.

She had just put her bag down, put her head down, moaning, "Will I be out here all night?" when lights screeched near her. Jerking up straight, she stared that way, gasping, "Oh, God, this's

65

it," and got ready to run. Anywhere for as long as she could. Until the last minute, not giving up. The car rolled slowly up to where she was. She froze.

"My goodness, child," a woman's voice said, "What're you doing 'way out here this time of night?" Inside the car the light went on. The woman, who was brown-skinned, about Jean's color, had her head out the window. She looked refined and was pretty. And the man who was steering the car was fine-looking and brown-skinned and portly. "Get in. We'll take you to Omaha. This's a bad place to be."

Jean opened the door to the rear and got into the late-model comfort. "I'm so happy to see you," she said flinging her bag and the sack of food down beside her.

The woman frowned back at her gently. "What on earth?" she asked.

"Someone stole my bus ticket," Jean lied.

"Oh, that's a shame. We'll let you out at the YWCA in town. Have you any money?" She was fumbling in her purse.

"No, please. You're really wonderful. I can pay for a room." The ceiling light went out and then the car was moving. Fast.

"Not such a good idea being out here," the man said.

"Oh, I know. I hated what happened," Jean sent forward. "You're from Omaha?"

The man said, "Yes, we are."

Without glancing back this time the woman said, "Good thing I saw you. My husband thought you were a deer."

"That's funny." Jean laughed settling against the seat, tired but no longer aching. "Me a deer."

Chapter Seven

She felt safe in the car. The man who was about forty, very little older than his wife, wanted to know how far she had come. She told him. Did she have any relatives who might wire her some money? "When I get to Omaha," Jean lied, "I'll call my sister long-distance."

"I certainly would," advised the woman, "Because you don't want to be out here like this as much devilment as is going on. People'd as soon kill you as look at you."

"Don't I know it," Jean said, because there wasn't anything else to say.

"Seen a few girls out on this road," the man told her, carrying the car forward smoothly, "but you're the only colored."

"Guess there aren't many of us," Jean told him.

The woman laughed gently. "Never can tell. You might be another first." Jean laughed and said she didn't think there was much credit in that.

It didn't take long to get to Omaha. The city had bright lights and wide streets, a good many cars going and coming, pedestrians roaming that resembled people back in Des Graces. Some of the buildings went fairly high, taller than Des Graces's, nothing like Chicago's. "Civilization," said the man while Jean was staring through a window.

She said, "Pretty big isn't it?"

"Oh, yes indeed," the woman admitted over her shoulder. Her eyes slanted up at the corners and when she talked, her top lip curved slightly over the lower one. Light sketched Jean's dilapidation. She was ashamed. The woman looked so stylish and a man was there. Neither of them seemed to notice how she looked.

The man said, "This's the real gateway to the west. Leave here and there's nothing for a lonnnng way." He drove several blocks to a four-story brick building barely off the main street, its purpose verified by a big neon sign. "They don't charge much here," he mentioned. He was a big man, wearing a small moustache.

Jean smiled, "I really appreciate this. You'll never know."

" 'S all right," he smiled back.

Taking hold of her bag, Jean left the car. His wife said, "You're entirely welcome. Hope everything works out."

The air was warm and the place well lighted in front. Jean went inside and up a half dozen steps to the desk, afraid they might be filled. They weren't. It cost her five dollars for the night and a dollar deposit for the key. The lady behind the desk was pleasant. And where were the bathroom and laundry? "On the same floor, middle of the hall." She pointed left toward the elevator. And she promised to call Jean at eight aye em.

Jean rode up to the fourth floor, relieved that the place was clean and comely. Her room was three tired steps to the right. It was nice, not large but comfortable. Unloading, she caught sight of the dirty girl in the mirror, gasped, "Ghastly," then sprawled on the bed for a minute enjoying its softness. Not much later she transformed her clothes in the automatic washer and dryer, and then soaked away Iowa. After that she counted her money. Three dollars and thirty-four cents. Plus the dollar key deposit. That meant cashing her traveler's check the next morning. Starving, seeing the cheese was too old, she ate dry bread and a warm apple. Some of her hunger went away. "Civilization," she said to the pastel room, "it's got something to recommend it." There was a facebowl with a clean glass on it. She drank three glasses of water, and then consulted her maps. Iowa went into the trash can. On the full map she lengthened the line before folding the bedding back.

She slept until the buzzer sounded, and got ready for Nebraska. Finishing the fruit and bread, she left the little room like someone leaving home for good. Downstairs she retrieved her key deposit and tried to cash the traveler's check. A different lady was at the desk, just as pleasant. Apologizing, she said they didn't take them. "But they're good anywhere," Jean insisted. The lady was sorry.

Glumly, Jean asked if there were any grocery stores open around there. There weren't. Wandering away to the main street she caught a bus to the town's west seam.

Nebraska along U.S. 30 was crowds of runty hills covered with dead stubble. It was treeless and houseless and full of rattlesnake holes, a long, hot, lonesome land that overdid itself. The map gave no hint of how many turns of the wheel it took to measure the width of it. No map could have been big enough. Besides, it called for a map of feeling . . . All bad. Jean burned, ached, starved, and suffered, begging for a gas station or even a bush.

A sheriff gave her a short ride to what he said was a better place to wait. And right away a Nebraska man lifted her thirty-five miles. After that, the angels worked slowly. At a down-at-the-heels restaurant five inches across the map she ate a bag of potato chips and drank a soda, and was still hungry. When she asked to cash a check the owner scowled, and she thought at first it was the way she was dressed. And then wondered if it might not be something other than that. She used his obscene toilet. Out on the road again she sailed her thumb.

An empty-eyed, line-lipped farmer rattled her forward a trace, never troubling her with talk or a paw. "Keerful," he warned, going away, "ther pickin' 'em up at Grand Island."

Jean guessed he meant prostitutes. And it set her thinking. Were there many out here? And how was business? Except for that sheriff she hadn't noticed the law cruising around. And what kind of place was Grand Island?

Favors helped her crawl across the plain. And late in the afternoon a cross-country truck braked, and a team of two men said they were headed for Denver. Denver sounded good to Jean. She got in between them. The man at the wheel was youngish and shoddy-looking, worn out by the road, without much outlook or flavor. He had sandy hair and a bottle. And before the truck had gone very far, his head was back and he was gulping. The level of the cheap fifth went down two-thirds before he reached across her and gave it to his friend. The friend was much older and bloated in the midsection. He drank half of what was left. Both of them kept giggling and guffawing like something was really funny. The old man offered the dregs to Jean. She told him she didn't want any. Her bag was on top of whatever they were hauling and covered with a tarpaulin. Her mind was on it. The gas gauge registered nearly empty while the thin man at the wheel grinned, full. He giggled in winey Alabaman that he had to stop at Big Spring, "fer gas an somethin' t' eat. 'N' 'en we c'n go on t' Denver. Y' with us, ain'tcha?"

"Yes," Jean said.

Big Spring wasn't very big. The edge of it had a railroad yard near some picnic tables, a restaurant, filling station, and jail.

While the two men were eating, the sky grew dark. And in front of the crammed place, Jean read the stars. When she went inside, the old man had finished and his partner was close to finishing. She asked for her bag. The younger man turned pale and stopped swallowing, but he didn't move. "I said, give me my bag." Quietly. He wouldn't answer, looked mean eating again, tyrant to plans that included her, willing or no. "I want my bag. Give it to me," she tugged, afraid to talk loudly. Afraid. He only opened his mouth, put full prongs in, chewed what was on them, looked meaner. His friend let a thought go down his own throat, and lowered his small myopic eyes, looking ashamed or bitter or both.

"Give her the bag," he urged softly. Age counted. Sulking, the other trucker got up and shuffled out slowly. Jean and the oldster went out behind him. Beside the truck he balked again, was told, "Give it to her." Glassy-eyed, jerking his shoulders, the man who'd had the plans snatched out the luggage and set it roughly down on the dirt. "Let's see if we can find someplace round here to stay overnight," his partner told him gloomily.

" 'Kay," he mumbled wasting the smell of his wine in the air. Then he sulked off beside the old man who seesawed on one bad leg to wherever they would be sleeping.

Not feeling good, following all of that, Jean snubbed the fifth-rate food and walked toward the picnic tables and put her bag on a bench attached to one of them. "What a place for an outing," she said, trying to laugh and relax. "Railroad soot, crummy scenery." For a few beats of the pulse she sat beside what she owned until the somewhat faraway sounds at the truck stop left the air. Imagining that all of the men in that dreary lean-to had gone for the night, she thought about trying for a money trans-action and decided against going back. "Somebody'll cash it," she believed. An engine whistled, snarled out of a building, and rolled on. "Good grief! What a racket. I'm glad it's gone."

Every fifteen minutes another engine shrieked and thundered in, then out again. She lay down on the table touching her bag with her hand. Nebraska had worn her out. She craved sleep. Footsteps came near! She jackknifed up and stared all around, saw three shadows. Men. She leaped off the table triggered for a scream. The men stopped where they were and backed away slowly, stopped again thirty feet from her. She was ready to run. Suddenly, they went away.

It dawned upon her she hadn't been breathing, and she started again. She crept back onto the table, sat up briefly, cautiously lay down. An engine clamored. Owl-eyed, she scanned space, then lowered her lids.

Noise!

From the same direction. Closer. She sprang up again, and hissed, "Get away!"

"It's a nigger," said a shadow.

"Ain't but one a her. Come on." They started toward her. She caught hold of her bag.

A light shot her in the back.

She snapped her head around. Saw the jeep coming. The men ran fast, scattering, getting lost. Near now, the jeep stopped and the man who was in it climbed out. He was tall and straight and wonderfully built, and he walked toward her, showing a sun-tanned, chiseled face. And his confidence passed easily for masculine beauty. She guessed that he was going on forty. The five-gallon hat he wore and his long-sleeved shirt and trousers were light gray. Black boots barely showed from under the cuffs. On his hip was a gun in a belt. He talked low. "What're you doin' here?" He didn't seem mean.

She noticed the silver badge on his shirt front. She said, "I'm hitchhiking." And mentioned about her bus ticket.

72

"Too bad," he grinned. He didn't believe her. "Those men spookin' ya some?"

At first she didn't know what he meant, then guessing, said, "Maybe they were just curious."

"This isn't a fit place t' sleep. Come on over to the jail," he offered. "You can have it all to yourself."

Jean didn't want to spend the night in jail. But anyhow, the way he was pointing was beyond the railroad noise. She could see the brightly lighted little one-story building sitting by itself. Her instincts told her he wasn't interested in her. And if he had been, he wouldn't have used force. Even when he said, "And if you want to do it tonight, we can go over to my room."

"No," she sighed, fed up. She knew how she looked. She looked awful. And she knew out here the majority of men didn't care. She could have been a female alligator. As long as she could answer in soprano, they'd ask to go to bed with her.

He had a superior chuckle, deep, detached. And he didn't think she was bad-looking. He got into his car. "You comin'?"

She didn't move right away. She wondered, "What's it like at the jail?"

"Got a bed," he said, letting his voice lope. "Two, matter of fact. You can have your pick."

"I mean the office," she pulled. "Any place where I can sit?"

"Sure. My chair. I won't be botherin' you . . . Unless you want." He didn't think she was bad-looking at all. He just wasn't one to stalk and wrestle. Her princess air made him grin. He'd never seen a nigger princess before, he kept thinking. It was something to watch, wearing the wrong clothes, in the wrong place. Kind of funny.

Pretending to make up her mind, she made him wait, then said, "Okay. Be better than that horrible noise."

Scared to be scared, he was thinking. "Get in." He palmed the seat beside him.

"Rather walk," she said.

He laughed. "Sure you're not for doin' it?"

"Course not."

He laughed a little louder as if he didn't give a damn.

At the jail, she went in. There were two cells fronted by a desk and two wooden chairs, one larger and more imposing. An overhead light was helped by white walls. Lacking tenants, it looked bleak. The sheriff was out of the car. "Go on in. Right in there if y' like." He moved his large strong hand toward a cell. She recoiled at the thought of putting herself in, of sitting in a cell again at all. Cook County throbbed up. She shook her head. "I'll sit in a chair." Besides, the mattress was filthy.

"Suit yourself," he drawled. "Well, get a good night's sleep."

"You too," she told him loftily. He chuckled and left, leaving the door open. "He could've knocked my head off if he'd been mean, the way I talked," she told herself. Just the same, she was mad. "Didn't want me and still asked. He was just playing with me." Going over to his chair, the bigger one behind the desk, she sat in it and put her head down, tired, letting her hands hang limply over her knees.

Bugs!

Thousands of them all over the floor. So many kinds she'd never seen before. "I'm not going to sleep tonight," she whimpered. "Maybe I ought to go outside again." Then she remembered the three shadow shapes. "Well, Jeannie, what'll it be, men or bugs?"

She slammed her foot down. Small once living things lay squashed. And a floor full were still crawling around. She couldn't kill them all by daylight.

But anyhow, she could try.

Chapter Eight

She left the jail early in the morning. The sheriff, she imagined,
was still sleeping. She wanted to get away from Big Spring, leave
Nebraska, and throw away the map. Because she was tired of it
and hated it. There was only a little bit left. The jail didn't have a
toilet or any place to wash up, and no drinking water. Stiff and
sore from fighting all night she creaked across the yellow dust to
the truck stop. It was closed. But there was a trucker out front
ready to go. He was a young man and said he was heading for
Cheyenne. That was farther west in Wyoming.

He had charge of a diesel and it moved pretty fast over hot and
hilly and desolate road. Going along with him, she couldn't tell
when they crossed the state line, the land looked so much the
same, there weren't any lakes or streams or animals easing the
ruin. To the west the squat hills were purple. Now and then the
wind cued tumbleweed across the swells in front of them.

Wide miles apart were Little America signs, and she asked the
man what that was. He told her without color or flavor, "Wait'll
you see it."

In front of an isolated greasy spoon, a girl was standing on the
other side of the road. Her long black hair was slinking down her

back, and she didn't have her thumb up. Just stood there waiting, a pretty girl wearing a tight sleeveless sweater, slacks, and flats. Her bosom and hips ballooned her clothes and she carried a ditty bag. "See a lot of 'em out here," said the driver, who hadn't been talking very much. "Business ain't bad. She'll get picked up quick. Make good money. Guy'll let her have the key to his room. Pay for her meals and such." He had dull little eyes and truck pallor and was medium tall and slender, the kind of man who never choked his feelings. Just let them lounge around inside. "Sheriff don't give 'em no trouble in this state and west a here. Not 'til y' get t' California. Aw, they're tough on any kinda hitchhiker." And then he smiled to himself. "Two things y' cain't bring inta California. Citrus fruit and pussy."

No hitchhikers. Jean took that personally.

He stopped the truck, and they both went into the building, each for different reasons. The last thing she did was ask for water. And the meaty tough owner sloshed some toward her. She gulped it, and went out to the cab again. Her traveler's check hadn't been good there, and wouldn't be anywhere in Wyoming. "This's got to be over soon," she grumbled to herself, fed up with being empty and broke.

And she couldn't flaunt her thumb in California. Where could she catch a low-budget bus? She jerked out her U.S. map, and her finger rode it west for a space, then south to Salt Lake City, and west again to Reno, Nevada. Of course. It wasn't far from San Francisco. Would they take her much-snubbed check at the depot? Lord, they had to. They *had* to. All right, Reno.

The driver didn't take long. He climbed up and into the cab, putting a paper sack between them. "Eat it," he told her. And when she didn't take it on signal, "It's good. I don't want nothin' for it."

76

She peeked in. Hamburger and soda. "Thanks," she said, taking out the sandwich first.

"Know y' didn't get nothin' in there, and last night didn't see y' get nothin'."

"When did you see me last night?"

"I seen ya."

She took a big bite. It tasted so good. And was gone soon. They had already begun moving again. After drinking the soda, she told him it was nice of him, and he flicked that away, jutting his lower lip and wrinkling his forehead. He wasn't a bad-looking man.

The stretch to Cheyenne was covered. She saw only the pastel edge of it. He let her out and drove on. Thinking about Cheyenne, feeling fairly good, "When I get a house," she said out loud, "I'll paint it, steps and all, pink."

Five rides shifted her to within twenty miles of Laramie. Once a man U-turned and tried to pick her up, but she saw that act and told him so. He looked insulted and drove off fast. A big truck took his place without missing a beat. And the homely, bumpy little trucker who didn't have many teeth said he'd keep to this road going into Little America with a stop overnight in Rawlins. She found the first near the other side of the state. She told him she'd go as far as Rawlins. It was a huge truck hauling furniture from St. Paul. On the way he talked about dirty-minded men, "like that feller back there. I seen 'im," and what a different sort he himself was. "Don't think a nothin' seein' a woman 'cept what she's got under her clothes. I ain't that way and don't intend to be." He never got off the subject. His hat had seen a fair amount of trouble and hid gray hair. The little he had in the way of a mouth was off to one side. His voice was high and his eyes scaled to a needle's.

He bought her a meal at one of the rare near-mirages, soup and a toasted cheese sandwich that tasted terrible. But anyhow, she found a restroom and scratched off layers of two states.

He came out last, stumbling along on badly bowed legs, his dirty trousers hanging strangely loose in the crotch. His waist was thin and he swelled in the belly. She hoped he'd leave off the wicked talk. He didn't. Finally she told him she was sick of all that. "Okay," he said, "if that's how y' feel." A minute later, he was on the subject again. She was afraid of him.

It was late. Rawlins was near. The old man said she didn't have to get out tonight. That if she wanted she could sleep in the trailer. Lifting a flap of cloth behind them he showed her his own bunk, a single bed built into the cab. He said the trailer had pads inside and plenty of room. She was to think about it. Time they got to Rawlins she could make up her mind.

In the mountains there's no twilight. The sun goes down and it's black. The man just happened to mention there was no hotel in Rawlins he could think of. And if it was him, he wouldn't be hitchhikin' in the dark fer nothin'. But anyhow, she could suit herself.

Around ten thirty by his watch he ground gravel in a truck camp, a site as still as the highway. Other trucks were already parked there. She guessed there were people in them, sleeping. She looked at her dirty fingernails. Was he sure there was room in the trailer? He said, "Plenty. Got the furniture all tied in place. Left a wide space." She mustn't forget to put somethin' in front a the door.

Outside the air was sweet and cold. Stars sparked the high dome. She shivered while he unlocked the door in one side of the huge box on wheels. Then he held her bag steady and she stepped on it and higher into a blacker blackness. "Walk back a couple steps," he told her. "You'll feel a string. Pull it." She did and got pale yellow light, amazed at the space inside. Showing only to the chest, he hoisted up her bag saying, "Get a good night's sleep."

She told him, "Night," and closed the door, blocking it with her case. Turning around, she admired the view again. On both sides were thick pads held hard by ropes and leaving twelve bare feet from front to back. The ceiling was high.

"Change this stuff around," she said, "and I could have myself a house." A mat covering the floor felt soft enough for a bed. She sent her chest on an air ride and stretched. She was going to *sleep* tonight like she hadn't since Omaha. What a funny old man! Sure couldn't judge who was all right and who wasn't. Feeling giddy, she galumphed and sang, "Long ride, fancy hotel, Little America hah hah hah." The clowning wore her out. She reached up for the string and jerked. Blackness. She listened. Nothing. Sagging down on the mat, she closed her eyes. And slept.

For minutes.

Until the door creaked.

She bolted up, shouting, *"Don't come in!"* Blind still, her head spun. *"Stay out of here!"* Her heart hammered and she panted and her temples hurt, crying out loud, *"Get away!"*

"Give you ten dollars. Please. Just a half hour." A little voice. High.

Familiar. "Ten dollars. Come on."

"No! Don't you dare come in here! I'll hitchhike first!"

"You don't have t' do that. I'm sorry. Didn't mean nothin'. Okay? Stay in there. Won't bother you again. I promise. I'm sorry, hear? Y' c'n go back t' sleep now." The door closed, rattling the case. Steps went away. She stumbled over to that side of the trailer and pressed her ear hard against it. Maybe he wouldn't come back and maybe he would. Thinking. Hurting all over, she gulped air and was *mad* and weak and felt like cursing and did curse, at the same time trying to hear something, someone. No one was out there any longer. Unbelievably limp, she stumbled to the center and clawed the air, found the string, pulled it. There would be light until daybreak. Aching, she drooped farther from the door over to the mat and slid down, sitting with her back to one false wall. Ropes rubbed her spine. She stared across the space at more of the same, knots and criss-crosses. "He robbed me," she panted. "He robbed me." She beat the mat. And then sleep beat her. More than once she nearly went down.

Somehow she knew when it was daylight. Before the man knocked gently, calling to her. She was still sitting with her back against the ropes. Red-eyed, she said coldly, "Don't worry, I'll be out in a minute."

When she opened the door, a clear light textured the hills and plains, and the air was mild and still. The trucker took her bag and helped her down. "Didn't mean nothin' by last night," he said weakly. "Ain't goin' t' hold it against me, are ya?"

Everything looked different. "No," she sighed, "just so that's the end of it."

He put her bag in the middle of the cab seat. "No hard feelin's?"

"No hard feelings." Trapped in her aches, she got in slowly.

He hobbled past the front to the other side, hoisting himself. "Kinda shamed a that." He looked sheepish.

"It's okay," she said colorlessly, staring ahead. Three-fourths of the trucks had gone. He moved the stick near his right leg, put a bad-looking shoe on the gas pedal, and turned the wheel. They groaned on down the road.

For the rest of the ride he didn't talk and neither did she. Little America signs were bigger, more frequent. Wyoming looked bleaker. For a good while.

And finally he rasped, "That's it ahead."

Little America.

The town she expected was a way station, and outside it didn't rate hurrahs. Leaving the old man for good, she went inside the sprawling building.

And the world changed!

She stepped on billowing elegance spreading to peace and wealth. And perfectly cooled. And glistening and coddling. A woman smiled at her through a mirror. "Ever see anything like it?"

"Never," said Jean. Far from the door was a lavish room for queenly relief and bathing. For half an hour she hid herself, then came out cleaned and combed, drank some of the soft soda water, and floated on a yacht of a couch. A lady buoyed up beside her told her about a man who'd been down and out crossing the unwelcoming west a long time ago. "All this was a promise he made to himself," she gleamed. "Come as you please. And doesn't cost you a thing. Won't even let you tip."

Jean lounged for an hour, then went out to the misery and heat.

In a little while she was chugging west again in a truck that was lugging a load, and battling hills, and that, doing its best, didn't hurry. The brown-haired young driver told her about his wife and son and showed her their pictures. He'd bought food and coffee for later on that day. Seeing Jean's eyes, he gave her one of his two sandwiches. She ate it gratefully, taking big bites.

Miles apart, other public relations girls were posing along the shoulder, all of them wearing tight clothes, all pretty. Once the truck passed a soldier, another time a hobo. Jean hoped they'd get rides.

"I'm getting kinda tired," said the trucker. He'd been on the road five days and had fourteen hours sleep the whole time. First thing he was going to do was find a bed. Somewhere in Utah. "It's right around the bend."

More sorry-looking country, the brown-skinned girl was thinking.

Utah rose up! Swelled, flamed! Red cliff and yellow, the wind's work. "Beautiful," she said.

"I guess," he mumbled. "Seen it so much."

Birds looped and soared in the early afternoon light. She asked what they were. He told her, "Sea gulls."

She'd always thought of them as ocean-lovers. Finding them so far inland seemed strange. The Great Salt Lake, she guessed, attracted them. There weren't any in Chicago along Lake Michigan's fresh water . . . Maybe they were outcasts that had found the promised sea. She smiled about that, then heard them cry, and said, "They sound so lonely." The man didn't answer. Lonely, pulsed in her. And, outcast.

He took her as far as a narrow road winding south and let her out on gravel and hardpan. Strange and lovely stones were near her shoes. She picked one up and put it in a pocket saying, "I'll keep it." She wanted to take off her jacket. Had wanted to for days, but anyhow kept hiding her woman's figure, the clinging T-shirt. From another pocket she took out the map of the states. It wore a long line now. "Well, I've gone more than halfway," she said with her head down.

Across the concrete a young man was waving. She hadn't seen him come up and guessed he must have walked around the curve of the cutoff. There hadn't been any cars. His suit was wrinkled and he wasn't wearing a tie. She waved back. Looking both ways first, he came over to where she was. She didn't feel any fear. He had rumpled eyes and dazed hair, was taller than she and flabby. He asked her where she was heading, and she told him. "Lot of road yet," he said vaguely. "Just came from Las Vegas." He looked around at nothing. Didn't seem to see her really. Said to the wind, "I was winning." He'd gone into some casino with five bucks. That was night before last. "Got up to eighteen hundred. Shoulda quit then." He scratched his stringy brown hair. Why hadn't he? He didn't know. Felt lucky. Yeh. Thought, wow baby, one more run. "It was roulette, see?" Like that he'd have had over thirty-five thousand. He was hot.

"And what happened?" He couldn't stop. Just kept playing and playing. And quickly it was all gone. "Eighteen hundred dollars." Then he saw Jean and glanced down at his clothes, saying, "Gee I must look like hell. Been wearing the same clothes for two days," sighed, "well, got to catch a ride," and started back. "Good luck, hear?"

She told him the same. And before long a car came and took him away.

Chapter Nine

For three hours she sat on her case. That was twelve hundred miles in a plane, riding on fluff, eating a good meal, hating everybody in comfort. Up there in Heaven.

What was Ferris doing? Looking for her still? He'd never find her here, sticking out like a sore bum. She had loved him. And how had he really felt about her (thinking)? That last day was just talk, wasn't it? Or he would've said it before then. And after the way he acted in the store—nobody who loves you would want to hurt you like that. Anyway, what difference did it make now? . . . Seems like such a long time ago. How many days was it? Counting on her fingers—five. Is that all? Well! . . . San Francisco was sure a long way off. Especially when you're sitting still. With nothing coming your way. Or going east for that matter since that fat guy got a lift. San Francisco. What's it like? She'd heard big, bright, sophisticated, beautiful, liberal. Was it really? Or was that just "other pasture" dreaming? Lord, after all that wasteland, she needed a pasture. With a nice room and regular bus service. And a job. Would she get a job right away? "Oh, Jeannie, Jeannie," she said wanting to scream, "when the time comes, you'll find out. Doesn't make any difference what it's like. You're going there anyway."

Her shadow read six thirty. To rest her rump, she paced. Two cars whizzed by then, tail to the sun. She stared after them helplessly.

And then far down the road on her side a speck grew into an old sedan. She masted her thumb. The car whizzed by her . . . Screeched. Rolled backward. "Thank God," she laughed. It stopped in front of her.

Two men were in it. There were couples like them all over the West, kin to the territory by temporary adoption, surviving on railroad work or manna. They dodged the cities and their too familiar jails, drifting on six cylinders for as long as the gas lasted. The one on her side was big. The arm he grinned over had bulk without much muscle and a tattoo of a naked woman above the elbow. His good looks were the cheap kind capped with black curly hair. His brows were bushy, shading self-impressed brown eyes. He had thin lips and a small well-shaped nose, and a color as red as the rocks. The other man was thinner and smaller, too pale. He leaned over and gaped at her. It wasn't a bright gape. The big man said, "Kinda far out, ain'tcha. Where y' on yer way to?"

"Where are you going?" she asked him.

He spread his hands and squinted. "That ain't no kinda question, is it, Beakie?"

"Naw," said the other man. He had a high nasal voice.

"Here we're bein' gentlemen. Chauffeur y' any place yer heart desires."

"No," she said, suspicious.

"Aw, now, y' don't want to be here after dark. Y' could git raped. That right, Beakie?"

The other man said, "Yeah." She turned cold.

"Tell y' what. Now y' just let us take care of y'. I'll git out and you hop in between us."

"No. I don't want a ride."

"Hear that, Beakie? Maybe she don't like our company."
Beakie showed poor-looking teeth. "Aw, come on now. Don't be
like that."

"Let me alone."

"Girl, I told you to git in." She loped west and Beakie moved
the car up to haunt her.

She panted, "Let me alone. Go on."

"Aw, lookit 'er. Fixin t' foot it. See? Try t' treat a woman
decent and she shows y' her ass."

Beakie didn't say a word. Just steered and grinned. And Jean
started running, her bag beating her side. "Let me alone," she
puffed. "Get away from me."

"She's scared. My, my," the big man taunted.

Beakie said, "Hee hee."

"What say we make her ride with us. We don't care she's a
nigger."

"Naw."

"Tell me they're better. Never screwed one. You?"

"Naw."

Jean spun, held her bag in front of herself. "Don't touch me!"
she wailed.

The big man got out of the car. He was scowling. "Aw, come
on. Don't be that way. We ain't gon hurtcha. Just wanta take y'
fer a little ride. Don't give me no trouble now." He wrenched the
case out of her hands, said, "Here Beakie, ketch." The other man
reached out, took hold of it, and set it on the floor.

Jean told him, "Give me my bag!"

The big man grabbed her arm. She broke loose and dodged,
ran backward. "Playin' hard t' get, huh? Well okay, if that's the
way y' want it." He didn't run well. She scrambled down the
shoulder. He lumbered along behind in army boots yelling, "Run,

nigger, hee hee. I'm gon ketch y' anyhow and skin y'." She raaaaaaaaaaaaaaaan.

Until she couldn't run anymore.

He caught hold of her wrists. She fell down in the dust and kicked at him, huffing and puffing, "Let—go—of me."

"You kick me an' y' never gon fergit it," he warned.

"Let—me—go!" *pant pant.*

"That's right, getcha air. I don't want no empty tank," he said, looking up and down the road. Beakie was looking too, but nothing was coming. The big man dragged Jean. Her sneaker came off. She cried, "My shoe!" He didn't give it a thought.

Beakie grumbled up to where the other two were. "Want me t' he'p y', Lonnie?"

"Naw," his friend growled. "I c'n handle 'er. But she's a fighter all right." She twisted and thrashed, and Lonnie caught her from behind by the waist. Her arm flew up and he grabbed for it and leaned toward the car, sweating and cursing. She pulled away hard. She clawed his arm and flung her legs, loathing the feel of him pressed against her back. Her jacket came open and her T-shirt went halfway up. For some time dust and gravel exploded. "She's mean 's hell," Lonnie panted finally getting a tight hold on her. And Beakie opened the rear door. Twisting her arm high in back, Lonnie pulled her into the car. The old heap turned and crossed over, drove east for a piece and made a hard right, lifting powder on the south road.

A westbound sedan was coming, not moving fast. Jean rammed her head out the window and *screeeeeeamed.* Lonnie jerked her back inside. She struggled but it didn't do any good.

"Ain't she a mean one, Beakie?"

"Yeah."

"Say we go 'bout twenty mile. Then won't be nobody nosin' along interferin'."

Jean's nerves were in total revolt, firing fear. The highway was getting lost. Where would they take her? To a desolate spot far from all help? And then leave her there. No, she thought, no *no*. "Stop this car," she appealed to Beakie. He didn't pay any attention. "I said stop, do you hear me?" Nothing. "What kind of man are you?" She saw then, and stopped asking.

Beakie didn't drive very fast out of respect to his heap. And a few minutes later he noticed, "Car comin' b'hind."

"Let 'im go by, hear?" Lonnie said. "Road's too narrow t' be racin' in this old can."

"Take your hands off—me," Jean struggled.

Lonnie snarled, "Wanta rassle, huh?"

"Ow! My arm!" She screamed. He was twisting it.

"Hold still then." She gave up, hurting and helpless.

"Y' know 'at car, Lonnie? They ain't gon go by. Jest a-settin' on ar tail."

The big man looked out. "Well, it ain't the sheriff," he said, relieved. "Try goin' faster." Beakie bumped the heap along, not doing much better. "Can't you git no speed outa this thing?" scowled Lonnie, seeing the other not far behind.

"Ain't no sports car now," the man at the wheel sent back.

"Please, you're hurting my arm," Jean begged.

"Gon set still?"

"Y-yes."

"Okay then." Lonnie let go of Jean. And she rubbed where he'd held her, seeing how smug he was because he had.

Then Beakie whined, "Lonnie, ah swan, it's stickin' with us."

"Think they seen us back there?" his big friend asked him.

"Might."

Jean spied through the back window. The other windshield was about two hundred yards away. She couldn't see who was in it. "How much gas we got?" Lonnie asked.

"'Nough," Beakie told him.

"Well, keep 'er rollin'."

Beakie went another mile. "Here they come right 'long side,"
he mentioned. "Ain't goin' for'ard ner fallin' b'hind." He glanced
out his side. "Boy over ther's signalin' t' us t' stop, Lonnie. Thank
ah oughta?"

"No, you crazy bastard!" Lonnie growled jarring the front seat
with his fist. Beakie jerked his shoulders up for a second and, like
he was told, kept going.

The two cars jogged along together riding bumps and turns.
Around the tall proud hills the air dimmed. Streaks showed in
the sky. The birds had gone. "Railroad pass up ahead," Beakie
reported. "Hope we c'n git th'ough without no wreck ner
nothin'. Doggone fool's settin' t' mess us both up."

"When you go under," Lonnie commanded, "force 'em to the
wall."

Jean said, "Oh, no. Don't do that."

"Sure," he snapped, "they wanna play rough, we'll play rough."

" 'Kay," Beakie agreed. "Heyyyy, ther a-crowdin' in on us.
Heyyyy!" He slowed, put a foot on the brake, stopped, upsetting
the two who were with him, dead center of the underpass. He
just missed hitting concrete. Eight feet in front and angled
toward his left fender was the other car. And a man and a boy
came out running. The boy rushed to the rear and the man
grabbed the door keeping Jean trapped inside, and tore it open.
She fell out on hardpan, then scrambled up crying, and stumbled
behind him and off a little way. "They've got my overnight case,"
she wept. Beakie was scared. The man looking down on him was
six feet tall, three inches shorter than Lonnie. His blue shirt and
khaki pants were clearly covering muscle. And something in his
eyes and the way he stood kept Beakie from moving at all. "Lady
wants her bag," the man said softly, shifting in heavy shoes.

Lonnie stared at him. Jean looked once. A square-jawed man, his light skin glistened. He wore a blond crewcut and had steady blue eyes and his nose was short and slightly hooked. Between his well-formed lips were even white teeth. "Guess y' didn't hear me. Don't want t' tell yew agin." Beakie and Lonnie stared, he standing there straight and easy, nearly smiling but not quite.

"Don't see where it's no business a yours. She's with us 'cause she wanted t' be," Lonnie snarled.

"Sorta didn't git that feelin' the way she come outa yer car," said the blond man.

And Jean cried, "He's lying!"

"Now you look," Lonnie growled, crawling out frustrated and angry. "This ain't none a yer business."

The blond man drawled, "Lady don't have t' go with nobody she don't want to."

"Well, you ain't doin' a damn thing about it," snarled Lonnie, staring contemptuously at the other man's left side. Where an arm should have been.

The boy had come away from the tail. He was short, wide-eyed, and skinny. And his hair was a mite darker and longer than his friend's. "Kid," his friend recommended, "brang me a couple of them bottles a soda in t' car."

The boy drawled, " 'Kay," and galloped off.

"Gon beat ar heads?" asked Beakie, on his guard.

The man's calm way and alertness kept Lonnie from making fists. "Naw, jest want yer pal t' try somethin'." Grinning, the boy brought back two bottles and flipped one to his buddy who caught it easily, said, "Here," and handed it to Lonnie. "Like fer y' t' take off 'at cap without usin' nothin' 'cept yer bare hands."

Fearing judo or worse Lonnie didn't turn it into a weapon. He wasn't brave. Defend himself he would. Or maybe get a man when his back was turned. One who wasn't so confident. Wrestling a woman was different. Lonnie gripped the bottle and picked at the cap with his dirty flat nails. Picked and picked. The others waited. It grew darker. All shadowy, he struggled and sweated.

He couldn't get the cap off.

"Give it t' me," the blond man told him.

Lonnie gave it up cautiously and the other man caught hold of the neck of it and in one motion tucked it under his armpit. Without straining, in a second he had the cap off and lying on the ground.

"Makes it look s' easy, don't he?" The boy grinned, wiping his chin on his T-shirt sleeve, then taking the soda. Jean was thinking, Good grief! Solid steel fingers.

"That ain't nothin'," Lonnie grumbled, "after I started it fer you."

Beakie put on his headlights and made light inside the car, and then it wasn't so dark outside where the others were standing. "Show 'im the other one yer holdin'," the man told his young buddy. Lonnie took it and tested it making sure the cap was on tight, then gave it to the one-arm man. He did the same with it as he'd done with the first and as easily. Returning it to the boy he said, with Beakie and Lonnie grudgingly admiring, "Now ah ain't lookin' fer no trouble. Had t' fight m' way ever since ah's way younger 'n 'at boy ther. Never lost a one neither. Nossir. Only hope ah don't have t' fight now. Some a them guys thought 'cause they's bigger'n me—kinda like yew—" he eyed Lonnie.

The behemoth didn't move. He grumbled, "Beakie, give 'er the bag."

The smaller man hefted it off the floor. "Here. We don't want no parts of it."

"Git it, Kid," said the blond man. The boy obeyed.

Lonnie pointed toward Jean, "Git 'er outa here." She glowered back, hating him and the spineless man at the wheel.

"Would y' keer t' ride with us?" the blond man asked. "We're headin' west on thirty."

"Y-yes, oh, yes," Jean said without finding out how far he was going. She got into the back seat of his car, not afraid anymore, not crying. The boy gave her her bag. She rested it on the floor on the other side.

The man got in front again and took hold of the steering wheel. His teen-aged friend moved in beside him, gripping the bottles by their throats between his fingers. "Want one?" he asked Jean, holding a cold drink toward her. She nodded and took it. The man turned on the headlights, forced his car backward, made an about-face, and retraced its tracks. The other heap sat wheezing and complaining. "Hey," said Kid, looking back, "sonabitch! Cain't git ther car started. Wonder why not?"

The man chuckled and said, "Kid put salt in ther tank."

" 'Most a whole box. Hee hee," the boy giggled, then gulped some of his soda.

"Case they's thankin' a takin' off agin with y'."

" 'Em guys'll be ther a while."

"Oh, my goodness," Jean came out. "But how did you know?"

"It was Kid here," said the man. "We's comin' 'round 'at blind turn and we heard y' screamin'."

"But I didn't think you did."

"Yeah. Didn't pay it no mind," said the man. "Figgered y's jest lettin' out yer feelin's. Kid seed yer shoe an' the gravel all messed up. Musta been draggin' y' some."

"I'll say," Jean shuddered. "The big one."

Kid reached down in front of himself. "Here's yer shoe. Ah 'most fergot." He held it over his shoulder.

She took it saying, "Thanks," and put it on.

"Could tell 'ey warn't t' right kinda fellers. They hurtcha any?" asked the man.

"No. But I'm sure glad you came along," said Jean, tying strings.

"Yeah, when Kid showed me 'at shoe, ah sez b'lieve 'at girl's in trouble. Reckon we best go he'p 'er. Funny thang, U.S. 30 North 'uz closed fer construction, er ah'd of been up t' er. It's a mite shorter 'n 'is road. Course, don't make no difference. Ah ain't in no rush."

"Well, it made a difference to me," Jean murmured. "And what you did took a lot of nerve."

"Aw, ah don't know," said the man, talking low.

"Yes, it did," she insisted. "And are you ever strong!"

The boy turned around, on his knees then, resting his wiry arms on the back of the seat. "M' buddy's strongest man ah ever seed," he testified, studying her hard.

"Kid," the man told him gently, "offer the lady some supper."

The boy rattled a paper bag in the middle of the front seat. "Let's see, ther's lunch meat an' bread an' my'naise, plums—"

"Anything'll be fine," she whispered. He let her help herself. She took a piece of fruit and clapped together a sandwich, using a pocket knife that the man handed back without bothering to see if it was clean. Taking off her jacket, she put it on the seat beside her. "How far west are you going?" she asked.

"Tryin' t' git us t' Longview, Washington. Er 's fer 's we c'n 'til ar money's all gone."

"Ain't got much," said the boy.

"What'll you do," she asked, "if it runs out before you get to Washington?"

"What we been doin' time we left Indiana. Stop an' work some. Take off agin."

"Done good so fer," the boy said, grinning. " 'Is guy c'n do 'most ennythang."

"Know we c'n git 'cross 'is state. Ain't worried none 'bout that."

Later, they rolled onto the highway. "Well, here we go," the man promised. Go go go, thought Jean. I don't care where. The North Pole even. Because I'm not getting out on that road again tonight. She heard, "Say, they call me Johnny."

"And I'm Jean."

He repeated, "Jean." Then said, "Kid?"

"Yeah?"

"R'mind me t'morra when we come t' a store t' be shore 'n' git some salt."

Chapter Ten

Lonely on the road, they moved along steadily. Johnny didn't strain the car with hurtful speed. For an old one, it didn't pitch and toss on what was generally good surface, and kept silent. Jean leaned her head back and closed her eyes and laced her fingers on her eased stomach, realizing she hadn't closed her eyes in a car before this.

Moonlight entered and impressed. "Looks sorta spooky out ther," Kid said to her. "Hey, too much air on y'?"

With her eyes closed, "No."

He peeked around, seeing where her T-shirt bulged. "You okay?"

"Mm–hm."

Still looking. "Been hitchhiking long?"

"Four days."

"How fer y' come?"

"Des Graces. That's in Iowa. It's just a small town."

"Me 'n' Johnny's from a small town too." Gaping. "Vincennes."

" 'S nice down ther," Johnny came in. "Think y'd like it. Right on the Wabash River."

What did he mean, nice? she was thinking, opening her eyes,

95

staring at the back of his neck. She knew about Indiana and what they thought about black folks. Heard it all back in Chicago. She said, "Wabash River? The one the song's about?"

"Yep," he said, then sang, "On the banks a the Wabash ferrrr uhwayyyyy." He couldn't sing. "Hey. Want t' hear some music? Kid, turn on the radio. See if y' c'n git somethin' good." The skinny hand made a knob click. Something classical played. "'At ain't no good. Turn t' 'nother station." Kid got pop. "Ain't no better." Twirling patiently, turning the sound up, he brought in a low plaintive wail that fit the western night and the forlorn valleys and hills. "'At's hit. Perty good, huh?" She listened.

> "M' gal tol' me no. That 't was time t' go.
> An' ah knowed fer shore ah'd crah."

"Tex Jenkins," Johnny told her. "Shore c'n sang."

> "That she had no use fer a man 'thout shoes
> An' a ninety-proof look in 'is ah.
> An' ah knowed Lilly Bee warn't a-goin' t' marry me
> When she got 'er a railroad gah.
> Got 'er a railroad gah-ah-ahhhhh!"

"Shore c'n sang."

Jean said, "Lovely."

Several more plaintive souls came on and did their chores. "Aw, here's one a m' fav'rites. Jimmy Pincus. Used t' be one a the Culver City Slickers." He had rhythm and a guitar. She liked him some. On the second chorus the two in front groaned along with the record.

> "Don't shed tears in m' footsteps.
> A garden might grow in ther clay

96

Temptin' someone s' lonely
T' come in an' pine away."

"Why're they all so down in the mouth?" asked Jean.

"Ah don't know," said Johnny. "Hadn't thought nothin' bout
it. Yew sang?"

She said, "Yes. Wait, maybe we'll get one I know too."

After a while there was one, a pop tune changed to country
style. She joined in. Johnny stopped chorusing and so did the boy
who was watching her still. Feeling self-conscious singing alone,
she stopped. "Y' c'n sang real nice," he told her. "Ever take
lessons?"

"Uh-uh."

He crossed his arms. "Y' been t' college, ain'tcha?"

"Mm-hm."

"Ah c'n tell b' the way y' talk." He shrank inside himself and
turned toward the front and relaxed.

The car jerked.

"Oh, oh," said Johnny. "Does 'at ever once in a while. Didn't
thank she would s' soon. Did run 'er a mite hard ketchin' up t'
yew, 'n' them fellers." Rolling onto the shoulder, halting, he
climbed out into moonlight. She heard the dry crumb crunch of
his shoes on gravel. He raised the hood and peered in. The
natural light was no help. "Kid, gimme 'at flash in ther."

Opening the glove compartment, the boy grabbed up the
valuable and handed it out the window near him. Johnny probed
briefly, eerie in the beam. "See what t' trouble is," he said out
loud, reaching in. Pretty soon a satisfied look showed on his face
and he came back to his seat and drove away.

"That fast?" asked Jean.

"War'nt much wrong with it," the man drawled.

"Ain't nothin' Johnny don't know 'bout fixin' cars," said the
boy.

"Got t' git t' gas station 'fore long," Johnny reasoned. "Should be one d'rectly." They roamed, listening to more songs and news. A bass voice said, "Nine forty-five." Big-bodied trucks passed them, chugging up a rise. "Ther 'tis. Kinda thought 'twas time." He veered left, changing pace, and poised his car in front of the pumps. "Y' all c'n git out if y' like. Kid, see if ther's enny soda." He asked Jean what flavor she wanted.

She was opening her case and taking out dirty clothes, and said, "anything." Letting herself out, she went to the ladies' room, only a short way off. It was a clean place. She took a soapy washup and put on clean lingerie and a clean T-shirt, then quickly washed what she'd been wearing along with her other dirty things. She sneaked the damp but not dripping wad back into the car between her case and hip. The other two were already there. Kid gave her a cold bottle of orange. And then all their heads went back and their throats moved. Johnny finished his first and made the car go.

When Jean was able to put an empty bottle near her feet, she took out several damp pieces in the dark and flew two of them out the window on her arm. A bottle crashed. Kid's. "Hey, what's 'at y' got ther?" he asked loudly.

"None of your business," she said.

"'Ey, Johnny. Guess what she's a-hangin' out t' winder? Hee hee. A tiddy sack an' drawers."

"Well, I've got to be clean," Jean said. "And if you'd just act like you didn't see—"

"Why don't y' mind yer business?" Johnny told Kid easily.

And Kid said, "Tiddy sack. Hee hee."

"Cain't do nothin' with 'im," said the man. "Mebbe he'll grow out of it some time er 'nother. Ain't but seventeen. Ain't dry b'hind th' ears."

"Aw yeah? Ah drank this much whiskey night 'fore we left,"

said the boy, stretching fingers, "an' didn't git sick ner nothin'. An' ah c'n cuss jest ez good 's y' c'n an'—"

"Well, jest keep yer eyes this way—"

"Tiddy sack. Hee heeee heeeeeee." Kid's knees were pumping and he was holding his face at the sides.

"Cain't do nothin' with 'im."

"Well, he's harmless enough," Jean figured.

The boy squirmed around, on elbows again, watching the moon-kissed shapes shiver and flap. "Ah ain't harmless. Y' jest don't know me, 'at's all. Ah bin noticin' y'. Seed y' got a nice shape. Ah ain't missed nothin'. If y' didn't thank ah's too young, show y' how much ah know."

"Aw, stop," she yawned. "Tell me about Vincennes or something else or I won't talk to you anymore." Inside she was laughing, and seeing the back of Johnny's head, knew he was too.

"Back home ah's all time gittin' in trouble. Nothin' mean. Jest differ'nt thango. Right, Johnny?"

"It's yer tale," chuckled the man.

"Ah's the toughest guy in Vincennes. 'At's right. Ah mean—"

"Yaaawwwwwwwwwwwn."

"Don't b'lieve me, huh? Ah'm 'most a man. Ah might look young—"

"YAAAAAAAWWWWWWN!"

The boy bragged on, scattering feats like sand. When her clothes were dry, she lost feeling. And he said, "Doggone, thank she's asleep, Johnny."

"Guess she's right tard," the man said. "Be needin' some m'se'f 'fore long."

The girl didn't hear the car roll onto the shoulder a good bit later. When her eyes opened she didn't feel any vibrations. And then she saw the boy scrooched against a door but couldn't see Johnny. She thought, there's something wrong with the car again and he's outside, until she heard his breathing. Lying there not disturbing the purpose of the night, she gently touched the part of the front seat where his body was, felt the man weight, held her hand there. As long as she could.

When she woke up again, red light charged all the air, and Johnny was smiling over the top of the seat at her. "Hi, ther. Didn't mean t' wake y' up. Gon git goin' agin."

"You didn't," she shrugged, rested. Sitting up, she stretched and fired up with air. Johnny shifted around to the steering wheel.

"Ah seed y' a time er two. Looked back when y's lying ther. Ah's thankin' thangs, boy," Kid gabbled, one wishbone arm reaching nearly the width of the front seat.

"Awww, here we go again. Not the first thing in the morning, please," Jean said, laughing.

"Ah got me a good look. Johnny he's a-sleepin' fer dead an' y' was too. Ah couldn't do but so much a-settin' in a knot up here b' this winder. So ah jest filled m' eyes some. Boy, sure had fun." He touched his buddy on the shoulder. Johnny only smiled. "Bet y' look right good in a bikini. . . . Got a bikini?"

"Go to sleep," said Jean.

"Hey, Johnny," said Kid, turning to something else.

"Whatcha want?"

The boy made a noise with the flat of his hand. "Gittin' a mite hungry. Hope we c'n find a store 'n' buy some vittles d'rectly."

"See if y' c'n git somethin' on the radio. Take yer mind off food," the man told him. "Won't he'p none, thankin' 'bout it."

"How much money we got?" the boy wondered, doing his duty.

" 'Nough so's we c'n eat t'day an' buy gas agin."

" 'N 'en we stop, huh?"

" 'S 'bout right." The bright, fresh morning report said it was hot. The singing was peppier. Jean guessed that was the daylight mood. She thought for a minute about what Johnny had just said, and then took out her U.S. map and scanned it. "Have we reached Ogden yet?" she asked him.

He answered, "Passed through it last night."

"Funny, I didn't see it. Was I asleep? According to the map, we should've gone right through it."

"Took a cutoff few miles north," he told her.

"What's the next town on this road? I mean, one with a bus station."

"That'll be Boise, Idaho," said Johnny. "Most a these towns out here ain't n' more 'n couple dozen shacks a-keepin' company."

She sagged back against the seat thinking, what was that smart little piece about hopping on a bus if things got tough? She hadn't seen the first one. Knew now this wasn't a bus route. Not since Omaha. It was hitchhike or nothing. Dreaming sure was different from the real thing. Like, you could dream that when you got a notion you'd tell whoever you were riding with, "Take me to the nearest town." So, he had to change his course. What a joke! Look at Salt Lake City. The night before, they'd rumbled forty-six miles north of it. If only she'd thought in time, she could have shrugged off the terror of that kidnapping, pranced out into the black, wild desolation, and walked to town. Or maybe, she'd have been lucky and got a ride. With another Lonnie and Beakie. She asked Johnny, "Have we gone as far as Tremonton?"

He said, "Nope."

Beyond Tremonton, she saw a red dot without a name, where U.S. 30 South put out an arm that reached into Nevada. The dots on the arm were uncolored and far apart. And the big print read, Great Salt Lake Desert. She knew she wasn't in shape for any more shocks. Besides, Johnny was terrific. If riding with him meant bending a little more than a hundred miles north so she could go hundreds and hundreds of miles west, well okay.

In Boise she'd check on bus fares—from there and from Portland—and pay whichever would be cheaper. "If I could get a traveler's check cashed, we could go a lot longer," she said. She was hoping to sign it over to him, feeling his luck would be better. She trusted him to give her the change.

"Y' got a traveler's check?" Johnny perked up.

"Sure. For fifty dollars."

"Heyyy, lady," he said, "With fifty dollars ah'll git y' t' Portland and y'll have plenty t' spare. That'd put y' a mite closer 'n y' are now. An' don't y' mind, ah'll pay y' back."

"Oh, I'm not worried about that," she said, "just had so much trouble trying to cash it. Every place I went, nobody would take it."

For a few spins of the wheel Johnny didn't say anything. Then, "Well, when we git t' gas station, y' git it cashed." He sounded sure of himself, talking low and even the way he always did. Jean wasn't so sure.

They hummed through cooler canyons. Clean, plump clouds fondled the cliffs or moved without passion. Sea gulls were up and gliding. "Those birds," she said, "I love watching them."

"See a lot of them in Washington," Johnny said, going straight. "Hear 'em up high screamin'."

"Don't usually find gulls inland, do you?" she asked.

"Couldn't say. Guess not. Funniest bird. Up in th' air look s' graceful. 'N' 'en they git down on t' ground 'bout's clumsy a critter's y' ever seed. Got bad-lookin' feet."

"Never guess it, seeing them fly," she said.

The car made peaceful turns, hummed down deep, crested. And Jean wore Kid's stare all over her body, put up with his giddy talk. Johnny hid his notions. Jean wished he wouldn't. She liked hearing him say things, liked his voice. Though he talked funny in a way, he and Kid. She hadn't a trace of southern accent. That was true of most of the folks in Des Graces. But Caucasians, she remembered, were always going on about how hard it was to understand colored folks, because they "didn't speak English." If she'd let the radio lead her, she'd have thought all Caucasians spoke according to the script. And yet few of them did, and so differently from region to region.

She wanted to ask Johnny his last name. Except that she sensed that out on the road, first names were usually all there was.

A small store showed up on a rise. They all went in and Johnny bought breakfast, packaged cupcakes mostly, and back in the car he passed out equal shares that they ate moving.

Taking a quiet turn, they went a little way before the car had a fit again. The blond man angled it over and stepped out, looking back carefully. Raising the hood for a second, he poked inside patiently. For about a minute tension knotted his arm. She watched him, his unassuming face. Kid was staring at her. Then Johnny was back. Cliffs jogged, trotted, rushed. "Can't get over how fast you find out what's wrong," she told him.

"Sorta know what t' look fer," he said.

A little later, he told her that it 'peered t' be a station in front of them, and t' git her check ready, and took out bills of his own. She fingered her book from a pocket while the wheels changed sound, striking softer stuff. A tall sun-tanned man came up and asked Johnny, "C'n I help ya, mister?"

Johnny said, "Fill 'er up and check t' oil."

"Yessir!" Before long, the attendant quick-stepped back, smiling after "Three dollars and eighty cents." Paying him, Johnny wondered if he had any soda.

"All kinds. Bring ya whatever ya like."

Finding out what the others wanted, Johnny gave his order, receiving his change, and then asked, "Say y' take travelers' checks?"

The man smiled, "Yessir!"

He pointed back casually. "Well, the lady's got one."

The attendant stopped smiling. As Jean held the small note out to him, she saw him gulp. He jerked it out of her hand and snarled, "Got any identification?"

She said, "Yes," and showed him.

Without reading, he scowled at it and then returned it. Returned her check, barking, "Sign it!" She used her own pen.

The car made music from that time until he came back holding some bills and three topless bottles. After giving Johnny the drinks, he jammed two ancient twenties and a ten into Jean's hand. She smiled sweetly, expressing her pleasure, and got no answer. Johnny gave her orange. "I appreciate what you did," she said quietly as the other man stalked off and Kid was taking his due.

" 'S all right," Johnny passed it off, making the man grow small and disappear.

"Feels good having money again," she confessed. "Now when we get to a town, I'll buy all of us something to eat."

"Buy ennythang y' want fer y'se'f. Got a little money left. Ah c'n git a few vittles fer me 'n' Kid t' eat."

"But I want to," she insisted.

He said, "Naw." She let it go at that.

"Y' c'n buy vittles fer me," Kid grinned. "When ah git back home, tell ever'body woman bought me—" by turns he gabbled and glugged.

"Guess m' wife's wonderin' wher ah am 'bout now," Johnny supposed.

"Oh?" Jean came back.

"Yep. She's most likely out front lookin' fer me."

"How long have you been married?"

"Four years . . . Ah's married once a-fore. Got two kids by m' first wife."

"Do you stay away long when you leave home?" Jean asked him.

"Aw, not s' long," he dodged. And she knew not to ask anymore about it just then.

When the boy finished his bottle, he sent it flying through the window. Tall weeds caught it. "There you go again," Jean complained. "Won't be long before the whole country looks like a dump because of don't-care folks like you."

Kid leered like a goblin. "Gimme 'nother, do it agin. Like t' hear 'em crack up, doggone it."

"He's what they call a litterbug," teased the man.

"Johnny, when y's mah age, had a lot a girls, didn't y'?" Kid pulled, hugging the back seat like he'd fall off otherwise.

"Ah reckon."

" 'N 'en why y' keep a-treatin' me like ah'm a colt, sayin' ah'm too young 'n' everthang?"

"Y' are."

"Naw ah ain't, Johnny. When we git t' Longview, ah'll show y' what ah know, y' hear? Be some girls ther?"

"Shore."

"Well, soon 's ah meet one of 'em—'at won't take me s' long ah'll letcha see ah'm a man same 's you."

"All right."

"Say 'at like y' don't b'lieve me."

"Ah do?"

"Wellsir, y' sez y's a man when y's mah age. Ah ain't no differ'nt."

"When ah's yer age," Johnny told him, toeing the car along a downgrade, making the view lose texture, "ah's doin' fer m'se'f."

"J'have a woman then?"

"Ain'tcher business."

"But y' had a lot a girls 'cause m' ma sez y' did."

"Ah reckon."

When we git t' Longview ah'll show y' ah'm a man too, Johnny . . . Johnny? Y' b'lieve me, don'tcha?"

"Told y' since we left home y' cain't do everthang ah do."

"Ah'm gon show y'."

"Shore."

"An' y' promise t' teach me t' drive too, so don't fergit now."

"Ah won't."

The boy was up on his knees, his thin neck choked in a vein mesh, his eyes stretching pleading. Several times his unsubstantial fingers rubbed an itch from his sallow cheek leaving commas of color to fade into tallow-pale skin. "Johnny."

"Yeah?"

"Whatcha thank Mary's gon say when she sees y' brung me 'long with y'?"

"Same thang she'll say t' me. Hi."

"Ain't s' shore she likes me. Way she was last time."

"Wanted t' come, didn't y'?"

"Shore but—"

"Well stop a-gettin' yerse'f upset. Jest don't break nothin' this time," Johnny told him, and then told Jean, "Kid broke m' wife's watch when she's a-visitin' m' mother. Right after we's married. 'S' one ah give 'er. She didn't like 'at s' much."

"Give her a lot of presents?" asked Jean.

"Sometimes. Allus sendin' m' children thangs fer Christmas an' ther birthdays an' Easter. Send m' first wife money t' take keer a them reg'lar."

"That's nice," she said.

"Jest had t' come outcheer 'fore ah go t' the army," Kid cut in.

"Going soon?" Jean questioned.

"In October," the boy told her, then said, "Johnny?"

"Whatcha want?"

"S'pose ah's t' go t' San Francisco with Jean?"

The blond man chuckled. "Doggone, thank Kid's got a crush on y'," he said over his shoulder, and then, to the boy, "If she'll take y'."

"If you go to San Francisco," promised Jean, working a cramp out of her foot, "I'll head for Spokane."

"Heh heh," the man chuckled. "Come t' Longview, why don'tcha? Ther's nice folks ther. Everone's s' friendly. Ain't no snobs ner nothin'."

"Maybe one day I will peek in on the place when I'm traveling around," Jean said, just making conversation, thinking, that's the second time he's said something like that. First Vincennes, now Longview. Would they be nice to her and any other brown-skinned folks? Or did he just like to say things like that, letting her know how folks treated him, or fooling himself? If there was a Utopia for dark folks, wouldn't she have heard about it by now?

The car followed a white line for miles to a cool semiprotected place, quitting the struggle long enough for Johnny to put his head back and concentrate on easier things than navigating. Back on the concrete and after working a while longer, he said he had to lie down. "You can lie down back here," said Jean, shifting her case. "There's more room. I'll sit up front."

"Aw, 'at's okay."

"No, now come on."

He pulled over and stopped again. She left the car.

"Kid, git b'hind the wheel," he told the boy. "Be more room fer Jean." Kid obeyed.

"Why don't we change every few hours?" Jean offered. "Don't

know why I didn't think of that before. We could take turns in the rear."

" 'S good idee," Johnny said long after he'd thought of it and let it pass from his head. He was tired, Jean knew by the way he moved.

"I know how to drive," she mentioned, climbing in next to the boy and closing the door. "If you like, I can help out."

All he said was, "Naw. She's kinda touchy with strangers." Aching, he shook his legs, standing on hardpan, rubbed his shoulder, then got in where Jean had been and lay down. Right away he was sleeping with a knee hoisted and a leg dangling in the aisle, his arm across his middle. Kid sat feeling the curve of the wheel and looking at Jean while she looked out the window. In one place beyond the shoulder, rock roamed down into a valley, into vagueness colored with sagebrush. There were no animals. She tried to see water. There wasn't any. Trucks boomed by, bearing all the big companies' names, baubled with license plates.

Three hours passed.

Johnny got up and scratched sleep out of his hair. He smiled, still hazy, "Better git goin'." They all changed around.

Jean had a seat to herself again. She said, "Sleep sure makes a difference, doesn't it?"

"Man's best friend," drawled Johnny. " 'Fore we seed yew, come a fer piece. Been driven' stiddy since day 'fore yesterd'y."

"Good grief," she came out, her gaze on the back of his neck. "At that rate it didn't take long coming this far from Indiana."

"Didn't come d'rectly from Indiana," he told her.

"But I thought that's what you said."

"Stayed ther few days seein' m' friends and m' first wife, m' mother. Seed m' kids—"

"What are they, Johnny?" she asked. "Boys, girls?"

"M' girl's eight an' m' son's six." He sat a little straighter. "Ther mother done a fine job a raisin' 'em."

"You sound proud."

"Ah am. Thank more a them two 'n ennyone. But like ah's a-sayin', we been a fer piece, Kid 'n' me. Went t' Alabama. One a m' sisters an' 'er husband lives ther. He'ped 'em chop cotton. They got a farm. Was ther three weeks. 'N' 'en went over t' Texas t' see m' other sister 'n' 'er husband. He'ped 'em on ther ranch gittin' in hay. Stuff like 'at. Stayed ther two months."

"You've been gone quite a while."

"Four months," Johnny admitted.

She thought about that. "Your wife won't know you when you get back," she said.

His head moved. "Aw, ah called 'er a time er two while ah's gone. Called 'er at m' mother's in Vincennes an' ain't been s' long since t' last times."

"Couple days?" Jean wondered.

He said, "Naw, 'bout three weeks."

"She knows when you're coming home then?"

"Told 'er ah'd be home d'rectly." That was all he said for a while. The old sedan moved forward the best it could on the hills, averaging thirty miles an hour. It was still Utah. Jean didn't mind.

Chapter Eleven

The travelers ate the last of the cakes. Kid flopped halfway around and drawled over his arm, "Y' in back 'er." He had crumbs on his mouth.

His muteness had been such a comfort. "Talking to me?" she asked.

"Reckon."

"My name's Jean."

"Hey, Jean."

"What?"

"How much d' y' weigh?"

"That's not your business."

"C'mon, tell me."

"Don't worry about it."

"Y' ain't big 's me."

"Ha ha." Not laughing.

"Well y' ain't. Got a heap more in the hips, 'cause ah seed y'. But ah'm taller 'n y' an bet ah weigh more 'n y'."

"Congratulations."

"An' ah'm stronger too."

She sniffed, pulling the Utah map from her jacket that she had flung behind her in the window.

"Want t' bet?"

"No." She studied lines and numbers.

"Ah'm stronger 'n y' thank."

"Um-hm." Glumly.

"Ain't ah, Johnny?"

"Yer tellin' it," said the man, guiding the car around a sharp turn.

On his knees, the boy forced a knot into the upper part of his arm. "See ther? Feel it," he invited Jean. " 'S hard 's a rock."

"It's beautiful," she mumbled.

"Put yer hand right ther," he fingered his puny swelling, staring big-eyed.

"No, thanks."

Kid pouted, angled toward the front, sat down. "Johnny," he said, "ah don't thank she likes me."

"Shore she does."

"Naw," said the boy, "she wouldn't feel m' arm." He waited, his mood changing. "Ah'd feel hers if she'd let me. Hee hee. Doggone it, feel 'er all over. She's afeered a me, 'at's what 'tis." Jean made a face behind him, then put her head down reading the map again. "Reckon 'at's it, huh, Johnny?" Smacking the man's arm lightly.

"Dunno," was all he heard.

Kid passed his hand in and out of his rear pants pocket, blowing his nose on a wadded-up mess of a rag before putting it back. Sea gulls screamed, Jean watched them, a spare company sailing, soaring. "That's the kind of bird little children make drawing pictures," she said. "Even when they've never seen them. In a way it's kind of mysterious."

The boy showed her one eye. "Y' use too big words. Cain't understand y'. 'Sides y' talk funny. Don't know what yer sayin'."

And she thought, *I* talk funny, said, "I just said it's mysterious. Okay, strange then." She tried to let it go at that.

"Reckon ah ain't 's smart 's y'," Kid went on using only his lower lip the way he and Johnny always did. "Cain't read ner write too good. Only been t' third grade."

"Didn't you want to go any further?" asked Jean.

"Aw, ah don't know. Wasn't larnin' nothin'. Tried. Didn't make no differ'nce no way . . . Johnny's lucky. He finished eighth grade." The muscles in his face strained for something deeper to say. Nothing came.

Jean thought about all the ways he and Johnny said some of their words. Theirs wasn't a fixed language, though she suspected it had been spoken pretty much the same for at least a century, because it was similar to one she'd read in old books. "I'm dying to see a coyote, Johnny," she changed the subject. "Doesn't seem like you're out West unless you do."

"Aw, they won't come down," he promised. "Ther back a ways in them hills. Folks spook 'em too much."

"Ah know a joke," Kid cut in. He told it. It was dirty. Johnny laughed. Jean didn't. "Hey, 's funny warn't it, Jean?"

"No."

"Ain't no kind t' tell a lady," Johnny suggested, being sincere.

"Thought it's kinda good," Kid squeaked.

"Well nev' mind, y' hear?" The teen-ager stretched a kink out of his back for an answer. Wind troubled the car, set it jiggling. Johnny worked harder keeping steady. Clouds had got thick. "Hey, Jean," Kid said.

They were dark clouds. "Hm?"

"How old 'er y'?" Fully turned and staring again.

"Why?"

"Jest wondered."

"Oh." Reading.

"Tell me."

"Tell you what?"

"Yer age."

"Why should I?"

"Y' know mine."

"So I do."

"Yer older 'n me, ain'tcha?"

"Mm-hm."

"Two years?"

"Nope."

"Aw, c'mon."

"Why?"

"Jest wanted t' know, 'at's all. Don't keer 'f yer older. Ah could be 's good 's enny man y' could thank of."

"Oh, for goodness sake. One-track mind." He's a goblin, she said to herself. Johnny didn't say anything. Kid told another dirty joke, then made a racket and fell over and held his belly.

The wind turned giant and kicked the car in its side. With scenery far below, Johnny toiled at the wheel. "It's going to rain," Jean shuddered.

"Ah know," the man answered. "Hope it won't be s' bad we cain't git through it." Another tall climb was ahead.

"Want me t' tell 'nother joke?" The boy offered.

Johnny said, "Naw."

" 'S good one."

"What d' ah tell y' a-fore?"

"Better 'n th' other two. Hee hee." Johnny heard it. It was dirtier. Jean didn't think it was funny, either. But anyhow, Kid leaned against the door with his eyes closed and his mouth wide open, shaking.

Rain wet the back of his head all of a sudden. He jumped away from the open space, losing his laugh and quickly raising the cracked window. Everyone's window went up. Monster water came down. The air blackened. South of them lightning flashed

113

in a long ragged line. Then *Baloooooom dalooom loooo-oommmmmmmm!* The car was slipping badly. "Ah'm pullin' over," said Johnny. "Cain't see a thang. Hope it don't last too dang long." Utah drowned while they sat on the shoulder.

"Ah'm s' hungry," Kid said.

"Guess we all are," Johnny told him gently. "Ain't many stores 'long this road. Probably won't find none 'fore Idaho. Ther's a town wher we c'n stop." Thunder roared.

"Let's buy some good ole weiners," the boy begged creasing his forehead and looking eager.

"Ah reckon."

"An' buns stidda bread."

"Kid likes t' eat," said Johnny, brighter for a flash. His lone hand caressed hard curved plastic.

"We ought to get something hot. We need a solid meal after eating so many sweets," Jean put in.

" 'Spect yer right."

"Hey, Johnny, r'member Deannie Wooten. Ole freckle-face fat boy?"

"Shore ah do."

"D' ever tell y' about t' time me 'n' him's sayin' who could eat t' most?"

"Naw."

The little thin fellow in front let an arm hang over the back of the seat. "Wellsir, we's playin' 'round back a his house. An' he sez, 'Maw's fixin' beans 'n' corn bread an' m'lasses fer supper.' An ah sez, 'Yeah? Boy! Shore would like t' have some m'se'f.' An he goes inta his house—we's a-settin right t'er on t' back. Sez, 'Maw, 's okay if Kid stays fer supper?' She had a big ole pot a-settin' on t' stove."

"Miz Wooten cooked fer ten ever' time ah knowed ennythang

114

'bout it," said Johnny, "with nobody 'sides Deannie 'n' 'is sister 'n' 'erse'f."

"Yeah. Wellsir, ennyhow," Kid came in fast, anxious to get on with what he was saying, " 'is maw sez, 'Shore. He c'n set with us. Skinny ole boy like him ain't no trouble t' feed.' "

"Didn't know y', did she?"

"Does now. Time ah set down t' table she went t' other room fer a minute. 'N' ah sez, 'Deannie, bet ah c'n eat more 'n y'.' "

"What'd 'e say?"

"Sez, 'Naw, y' cain't.' An' ah sez, 'Betcha.' Boy, he's shore a hisse'f."

"Miz Wooten hear y' all talkin'?" Johnny asked him.

"Naw. A mite later she come in 'n' sez, 'Kid, y' he'p yerse'f. Eat all y' want. Hope y' like corn bread.' Sez, 'Yessum, shore do.' Hee hee."

"Whatcha laughin' at?" Johnny was enjoying the boy.

"Heeeeee! Shore caught ole fat Deannie 'at time. 'N' bet 'is maw won't tell me 'at n' more." The small waxen fingers hanging in front of Jean fussed with air. "Ate everthang in sight. Deannie only got one he'pin' a beans, piece a corn bread."

"Didn't leave 'im no seconds, huh?" Johnny prodded.

"Shore. Grease in the pot. Ah ate like a pig. Kept a-sayin' how ah's still hungry. Miz Wooten 'uz gittin' mad, ah could tell. But she wasn't a-sayin' nothin' 'cause she's showin' 'er manners. But ah shore tricked Deannie. 'N' after we's finished, ah sez t' 'im, 'Thanks fer th' eats. Better be gittin' home t' supper er m' mother'll be mad at me.' Jest showin' off. Couldn't eat 'nother thang. Hee hee heeeeeeee."

"That 'uz kinda mean," Johnny told him evenly.

"Ah don't keer," Kid sent over with a serious face. "Don't keer atall. Do it agin. N' tell y' what ah done after ah's outside 'at door."

"What?" Johnny kept things going.

"Farted. Right in 'is face. He's a-settin' on t' stoop 'n' sez ah's stuffin' like a dawg. So ah jest farted on 'im. 'N' 'en ah ran. Boy, he couldn't ketch me, he's s' fat." Kid giggled again.

Johnny looked behind himself, pretending sadness. "What must we do with 'im?" he tested Jean. She sent her head back and forth.

It rained enough for three states. In such a short time, soaking and saturating, puddling, muddying. "Hope we c'n git outa here come time t' move," Johnny pondered, softly talking Jean's eyes up to his own.

Then Kid yelped, "'Ey Johnny, r'member ole Jess Bruner y' used t' he'p fix cars?"

The man faced the boy. "Course ah do," he said.

"R'member 'at song he's all time a-sangin'?"

"Yep. Only knowed one."

"How 'bout me 'n' y' sangin' 'at while we's settin' here?" He started,

"Ainnn't got nothiiin' ah call miine."

The man joined in,

"Wet 'n' chilleee half t' tiiime."
Gotta leave home.
Jest gonna roam.
Cryin's no good, prayin' neither
When y' git 'at wanderin' fever."

Fascinated, Jean watched them both hauling the tune between them, their necks exerting unmusical music, their upper lips not even trying, rhythm volleying between their gazes, face to face.

116

"What's 'at other verse?" The boy coaxed.

"Go wher y' c'n an' leave yer own traces," Johnny went along alone for a line.

> "Don't seek yer fortune in other men's faces.
> Only thang pays is makin' yer way.
> Wander by desert, highway, er stream,
> Heaven he'p y' follerin' a dream."

It was over, Jean was sorry. They gave each other a satisfied look, the man and the boy, then slowly turned away from each other, seeing the rain was slacking. *Spladatat splat tat* was all the force worrying the panes and steel carcass. "Guess we c'n go on ar way," Johnny grunted clearing the ardor of song from his throat. The motor soloed.

Jean murmured, "I like that."

"Kinda fits thangs, don't it?" Kid half whispered. And before she could answer, changed, baring his teeth and perking, "When we git t' town, first thang ah'm gon do's drank a ocean fulla water. Ah'm s' thirsty. Why, ah ain't had t' piss. Ain't got 'nough water in me t' wet the inside a m' mouth."

"Hold on," Johnny said. They climbed. The sun was out. They hadn't waited long.

Chapter Twelve

They curved under a vacuumed sky. Johnny sped through a canyon, except for the hum of the car, having quiet for company. All at once the road was wider, brighter. On Kid's side a stone fence formed a cove for a large number of automobiles and crowds of people, families mostly, sniffing the west. Johnny slowed, read a sign, "Highest point in the state a Utah." The land came to life differently here. It was greener, clotted with trees. "Want t' git out 'n' see what's what?" he asked.

"Sure," Jean said. Kid was already opening his door.

All of the others were city people, Caucasian and clean, pleasantly cloyed with the middle life. The small black car looked out of place, and so did the blond man and the boy in their poor rural wear, and the brown girl togged in rough clothes. They weren't ostensibly noticed. And if Johnny felt self-conscious, he didn't let it show. At first, Kid stood pigeon-toed, shrunken and silent near his friend, his hollow rubber hands at his sides. Before long he saw an angle he liked some steps away, and his feet made a weak commotion, going over concrete.

The slant of the earth beyond the popular fence was almost sheer. A long rutty fall full of weeds. The man from Indiana put the flat of his hand on stone and peered far into space relaxing his concentration. And Jean stared at the vast irregular view, glad for the chance to be tourist, though ashamed of the way she looked. But anyway, since no one seemed to care, and knowing she wouldn't be seeing any of these souls again, the feeling slid off down the mountainside. She was on Johnny's left near a one-story human wearing rompers, a boy who was begging to see. His father, a smooth-faced, black-haired man, lifted him up, shoulder high. Jean smiled at the child's face, Utah reflected, the tiny mouth opened, the eyes round.

Kid wandered back just then, grinning, and said, "Hey, Johnny, what if ah 's t' jump off?" Loudly enough for others to hear.

"Be a long time landin'," the man said calmly, seeing eternity below.

Kid put his elbows on the edge and frowned over the side. "Jest t' same be somethin', huh, 'f ah put m' arms out 'n' went flyin' out t'er?" Johnny chuckled. "Give everybody here somethin' t' talk on after they's home. Ah'd jest stand up on 'is ledge an jump straight out—"

"An' bust yer head wide open," said Johnny. "Come on. Time we's gittin' 'long." He started toward the car with Kid still jabbering.

"Bet ah could Johnny . . . Might not t' first time—"

"One time, wouldn't be no more."

"Y' don't know—" grinning because folks were looking at him.

"Reckon ah don't," Johnny agreed. "An' don't aim t' find out." Jean thought Kid sounded so silly. She was disgusted. Even the little children were acting like they had more sense.

The trio took their places, settling in. Kid gabbled faster than the wheels could turn. Until he noticed that Johnny wasn't listening, and Jean had her eyes closed.

119

"Made it t' Idaho," said Johnny.

Jean said, "Sure took a long time crossing Utah. Guess one reason's, after Wyoming, looked like I'd never catch a ride."

"Reckon we stopped a heap too," Johnny said. "Sleepin'—times m' car stalled—an' gittin' gas an' stuff."

"But that was fun," she whispered. Neither of them mentioned the kidnapping, though she thought hard about it.

The scenery changed. Satellite to the view, Jean wriggled around, put her back to one wall, blind to the eastbound lanes, and stretched her legs out on the seat. Feeling found all the numb joints. The sedan slowed. "Construction up ahead," said Johnny, his finger showing no agitation. Other vehicles waited too. Red lights hung on wooden horses. Men, naked to the waist, found high and low angles, riveting and shoveling.

On the outer lane, a boy wearing western clothes got out of a pickup truck, leaving a man inside next to the driver's seat. The boy, who was about Kid's age, was tall and strong. And he was handsome.

He set a sure squint on the work going on in front of him. And standing straight with his legs a little apart, he raised his elbow and took hold of his brim. His thumb went underneath, his fingers on top. Jean was thinking, just like the movies. Cars began moving. Their car. Kid ogled the cowboy whose pose had changed, then spat out the rottenest name in his throat. Sent it flying in its own juice. The victim froze with one leg on a shadow and his hand on the door of the truck. Cursing, he wiped his face, it boiling. His lips went inward. He got a good look at Kid. Captaining the car forward, Johnny frowned a hint. "Shouldn't a done that," he said, hardly raising his voice. The victim, having a slower start, fell back.

And Jean snapped, "That boy didn't do a thing to you. What'd you do that for?"

"Aw, ah don't keer. Jest felt like it, 'at's all," Kid said.

"Ain't no way t' act," Johnny mentioned, still frowning, not getting an answer. Jean looked from his back to the boy's, shocked and angry. Didn't Johnny ever get mad about anything? What did he want, a puny little yes-man? A mean retarded adolescent tagging along, all the time looking up to him, telling him he was wonderful? And what was wrong with Kid? What was wrong with him? Couldn't Johnny tell that something was?

Speed such as the small car could manage took them to Burley, a small town in Idaho with a supermarket. Because of other cars clogging the front, they parked half a block from it on the main street that hadn't much in the way of bustle. No building cared to go higher than two stories. Most settled for one. There were trees showing beyond the street, and dim mountains beyond where the town stopped. The few men, women, and children on the sidewalks kept to slow gaits, without tension, wearing plain clothes, not minding the heat. They were lean, their coloring was healthy.

The supermarket sold a good many items. In front of it were fertilizer, bags of seed, a number of farm tools. Signs invited through the glass with prices lower than the ones back east. Back east! Jean hadn't thought about it. About Chris, or Bernie . . . And Ferris. Ferris, Ferris. Ahead of the others she walked through his face into the store.

Inside it was cool. "Feels nice," said Johnny, taking a step forward to where she was. The boy lagged behind. There were lines of shopping carts. Johnny took one, pushed it toward the first of the hospitable aisles. "Come on, buddy," he called back to the boy.

"Ain't fer," returned from several yards away. Jean heard his wishy-washy clump.

"See ennythang y' want 'sides wieners?"

121

"Not yit." Johnny picked up six bottles of soda from a shelf. Jean went across the tile and frowned at fruit. "Say, got a idee," he told her. "Up t' road ther's a woods. Got t' rest some'ers t'night. Could build us a far 'n' roast wieners 'n' thangs. Maybe sleep out. Got plenty blankets . . . Er maybe y' don't want to."

Jean felt a tomato. "Sounds wonderful," she told him, putting some of the produce into the cart.

"Kid?"

"Whatcha want?"

"How 'bout eatin' camp style t'night if it don't rain?"

"Shore."

The man looked pleased with himself. "Better git some matches," he remembered.

Jean stuffed six big juicy apples into a bag, a head of lettuce. She and Johnny walked slowly down the aisle picking out what they wanted. Kid stayed behind.

When they reached the checkout counters the basket was full. One counter had only two other people waiting to be served who didn't have much. Jean stood behind them, Johnny was next with Kid last and empty-handed. When it was her turn, Jean took her packages out of the basket and arranged them on the counter. The clerk was a pleasant young girl, eighteen or so. She worked quickly. When Jean had gone through the narrow space, she noticed Kid looking scared and acting like he didn't know her. He was close to Johnny now. Johnny paid his own bill and asked for two shopping bags. And the clerk smiled at him while she got them from under the counter.

Then lugging both of them together by their handles, one full, the other about half, he came over to where Jean was waiting. Taking what she had, he forced it into the unfilled bag. Kid stood gaping around at other folks in the store, scared and tense. When his friend walked out beside the brown-skinned girl, darker after so many days of sun, he gave their backs some distance. Messed-up, nutty teen-ager, Jean was thinking, feeling insulted, not letting it show. After all that talk in the car. Johnny noticed, too, understood, and let it go at that. "Shouldn't take us too long t' git t' the woods," he drawled. "Ther's vittles we c'n eat while we's ridin'." He was the same as always. Jean put her hate away. Kid didn't seem worth it.

"It's him all right." The young cowboy was in front of the store next to an older man. Kid saw him before either Johnny or Jean did. "That's the little skunk spit on me and called me—" he repeated the filth—"out on the highway. Yes, I'm talking about you."

The eyes of the boy from Indiana scaled the near inches. He didn't look brave. "Warn't me," he lied.

"Oh, yes it was. I'd never forget you. And that car." The cowboy stabbed down the street.

"Jest a minute," Johnny started easily, setting down the shopping bags he was carrying.

"You stay out of it," the older man pushed in. "Little rat needs a lickin' doin' what he did." His face was craggy and middle-aged. A big tan hat hid the color of his eyes. He hooked his fingers in his levis. He wasn't a big man or tall.

Kid quaked. Johnny tried again. "Now we c'n talk 'bout this thang. He's man 'nough t' say he's sorry. Ah don't say he's right—"

"It's folks like him ruins things," the man barked. "He's no better 'n a dog." People stopped passing and made a crowd.

"Don't aim t' stand here 'n' swap dirt with y'. We'd best be goin'," Johnny allowed, keeping a grip on his feelings.

"That skunk's not going anyplace 'til I spin his brains around," the Idaho boy said.

123

"Come on, Johnny," Kid wheezed, "let's git outa here."

Johnny said, "Go on." Afraid to walk alone, Kid waited. "Jean, you go too." Upset, she obeyed.

"You ain't goin' to fight my boy," the man yelled. "It's between him and that little snake there." Taking steps, Kid winced.

"Ain't aimin' t' fight no one," Johnny explained.

The tall boy let Kid tremble a little way, then charged after him. Johnny ran. Jean coiled around, caught in the middle. The cowboy slammed her against a building. Someone in the crowd screamed, "Get the sheriff. Hurry up!" Kid yiped and spread his hands in front of his fright. The other boy grabbed one of his arms. Then Johnny's hand was on that one's wrist, ruining the color in his face. Kid was free and falling. "Dammit, take your hands off me," the Idaho boy strained. "You're breaking my arm!" Johnny let him go. Panting, the boy petted the red place. Jean was leaning against a door, holding her elbow.

"Now ah tole yew t' go on. Don't want no trouble. He's sorry 'bout what he said 'n' all. Ain'tcha, buddy?"

"Shore," Kid gulped, getting up.

"Sorry, hell. I'm going to tear his head off."

"Ah wouldn't if ah's yew," Johnny recommended. "Kid, git in t' car." The Indiana boy stumbled off. Afraid for Johnny, Jean waited.

"There he is," the cowboy's father was yelling sending a finger toward the blond man. He was talking to a giant wearing a badge whose big hat was gray and flat on top. The big lawman powered a gray shirt and trousers set off by a black leather belt and holder with a gun in it.

Johnny didn't move. His face was the same. "One's got that nigger with him," the man was saying. And Jean turned cold, hearing that.

"No sech a thang," said Johnny. "She's a lady."

124

The sheriff halted near him with his back to the crowd and the other man beside him. "Hit Frank's boy?" he asked.

"Naw," Johnny told him, "that ain't exactly right."

"Billy, how's your arm?" the lawman called out. And heard it was okay, then said to the stranger, "Suppose all of you get out of here."

Johnny said, "We intend to."

"Sam," barked Billy's father, "you goin' to let him off like that with no charges or anything?"

"Got no reason to hold him," admitted the sheriff.

"After what he did to my boy?"

The sheriff sighed, "Billy doesn't seem to be any the worse." Johnny went by him. "Hey, where you headin'? Thought I told you—"

"Mah vittles."

"Okay, hurry up," said the man in gray, and to his friend, "Calm down, Frank. They'll be outa here soon."

"Calm down nothin'," Frank seethed. "You're lettin' him walk away after he nearly broke my boy's arm?" The craggy man grabbed a shovel from in front of the store.

"Put that down!" the lawman shouted, running toward him. The thing made an arc in the air.

Jean screamed, *"Johnnee!"* He whirled and flung his arm up. And the crowd sent up terrible noise. The lawman lunged, grabbed hard, deflecting the weapon.

But not enough.

The edge of it crashed on flesh. Women in the crowd screamed. Johnny went down to his knees, head down and holding his fist against the front of his shirt. Blood splattered. Jean ran to him while the sheriff wrenched the shovel out of Frank's hands and pushed him away. Johnny swallowed, fighting awful pain. "Frank, stay the hell back, you hear?" barked the big man with the badge. "Everybody go on about your business!" People moved slowly. "I said get outa here!" Some did leave then. The victim rocked forward, swallowing and panting. Sweat and pain broke out on his face.

"Ohhh, Johnny, we've got to get you to a doctor," Jean half-whispered. Hot as it was, Kid hid in the car with the doors locked and the windows closed.

"Ah'm okay. Ugh—naw, naw—don't need—no doc." Blood dripped from inside his fist.

She pleaded, "but your hand—"

"Don't need no doc, ah said."

"Can't carry no bags now," Frank called out. "Got to let a nigger do it for you." Jean fought her own temper.

"Take it easy," said the sheriff, his jaw in a knot. "You okay, fella?"

"Shore."

"Aren't you going to do anything to that man over there?" Jean hissed pointing toward Frank, who was standing near the supermarket. The sheriff didn't answer. "I said, aren't you—"

"All of you, get out of here," he said showing her his contempt. As far as he was concerned, she was just another highway whore.

"Get the bag nigger-gal," the man called Frank was shouting. "Old one-arm skunk, he can't carry nothin'. Ain't man enough to carry his whatcha-call-'em? Vittles. 'S all right, one-arm. Hey, one-arm? Got a nigger-gal to carry yer bags!"

Jean, stiffened, despising the man, knowing she couldn't do anything about it.

"Frank, now go on home, I said. Okay, everybody, trouble's over." Official hands moved in the air.

The blond man was still on his knees. "Johnny," Jean whispered.

He said, "Ah'm okay." She reached for the bags. They were dead weight.

126

"That's it, nigger-gal!"

"Let 'em be!" Johnny shouted. Jean stopped. He struggled to his feet, stood for a second with his head down, then gulped a breath, another. His hand was still a fist losing blood. Blood stained his clothes in front. He sent pain down his throat.

"Johnny," she begged, "just don't pay any attention. I don't mind." Her face showed that she did.

He didn't look at her. His head went to one side and his eyes braked on the glare of the man who was taunting him. He sensed the crowd, strangers watching, not saying anything. He was staring straight ahead, and Jean saw something come into his face that hadn't ever been there before. From deep down. For a space he waited on the sidewalk. She waited, the sheriff, Frank, his boy.

And then the one-arm man clenched his teeth, opened his hand, and reached down. His fingers hooked around the handles of both bags.

"You can't, Johnny, you can't!" Jean cried, crushing her fists against her mouth. Lines stood out in his temples and along the sides of his neck. His arm strained. The bags left the sidewalk, and he began walking toward his car. She walked beside him with her arms crossed tightly over her middle, her fists hidden behind her elbows.

Frank kept silent.

The sheriff put his head down, let out air on his chest, and said, "Wait a minute, fella, I'll help you."

The blond man shook his head hard, walking and walking, passing the cowboy who was looking at him strangely. Red drops fell in a long line from a cataract darkening the side of one bag. He had only a dozen steps to go now. "Kid!" Jean shouted, running ahead of him, "for heaven sakes, open the door!"

Chapter Thirteen

Kid was on the back seat then, sitting with his knees pressed together. He opened the door, scared by the sight of blood on his friend. "Take keer a these," the man ordered, paler than he'd been.

The boy obeyed, setting them down on the rear floor, getting blood on his own hand. He wiped it on one paper wall, a plea on his daubed-in features. "Y' mad at me, Johnny?" he quivered, opening the door to the driver's seat.

Shaking his head, Johnny cleared his throat, with his hand free knowing less agony. Jean said, "Think I've got something we can tie on your hand until we find a doctor. Let Kid have your keys." And to the boy, leaking disdain, "Get my case out of the trunk."

"Take t' key outa m' pocket," Johnny said.

"Which one?" Kid asked.

"Right side." Kid dug in, sending nervous puffs of wind onto his buddy's back. He found the metal bunch and squinted around cautiously before exposing his scrawny frame to the street. The fellow he feared had gone. Jean watched him move toward the back of the car, with each step setting down half his weight.

The sheriff came up as Kid was forcing the key into the trunk lock. The boy jumped like he'd been shot. Ignoring him, the big man said to Johnny, "Say there, better get that hand to a doctor."

"That's what I was telling him," Jean said.

The lawman acted like she wasn't there. "Doc Sanfers on Linden Street. That's two over to your left. Middle of the block. He won't charge so much. Five–ten dollars."

"Thanks," Johnny told him. Kid hauled Jean's case to her. There wasn't any crowd anywhere. And the sheriff waved and went away.

"Got a white scarf in here somewhere," Jean said and found it. "Kid, you can put the case back." He did what she told him while she said to Johnny, "And, listen, I can drive. You don't have to worry."

"Give me m' key," he rasped, hurt still a film in his eyes.

"Want me t' put it in yer pocket?" Kid asked.

"Naw, in m' hand."

"But you can't," Jean protested, stunned.

"Yes, ah c'n."

"No, you can't go a mile like that." His mouth hardened. "Johnny, you can trust me. I'm a good driver. I've got my license—"

"Nobody sets b'hind this wheel 'cept me, 'thout ah teach 'em. And 'at takes a while. Won't go fer everbody right off."

"But we can walk to the doctor's."

"Ain't going t' no doc's."

"Johnny, you've got to."

"Ain't goin'."

"What's the matter?" Jean begged.

"He ain't got no more money," Kid said.

"Why didn't you say so? You know I've got some."

129

"Don't want y' t' pay m' way. Ah'll pay m' own way when ah c'n." He flared some.

"Don't look at it that way," Jean told him, folding the scarf over and over. "What if you get infection? And then couldn't use the hand at all?"

"If ah jest hold it tight 'nough the blood'll stop 'fore long."

"Let's see it," she said. Kid watched, not saying anything. Johnny didn't move, looking ahead at the darkening mountains. "Johnny, please." He waited. Opened his hand. "Ohhh, good God help us all!" Her hand went to his arm. He hid the wound again. She pleaded, "Johnny, you've got go and get that fixed. Take the money. It won't be much. The sheriff said so. Johnny?" She handled him gently. He yielded, sitting on the front seat, letting her bandage his palm and tie it around his wrist. Now his hand didn't punish him so much.

"All right," he promised, "but ah'll pay y'."

She went to the other side and got in next to him. "It's okay," she told him, relieved. Reaching into her bosom, she took out the money and put twenty dollars into his shirt pocket.

"Pay y' back 'fore y' git t' San Francisco." By some miracle, he started the motor. They went around corners seeing at last the right sign above a door and stopping. The man went in alone.

Later, he walked out grinning faintly and wearing proper dressing on his hand. "Doc's nice guy," he passed along. "Told 'im ah's driven' 'n' how fer. Put a pad 'cross t' front a m' hand t' he'p it some. Didn't charge me but seven dollars. An 'is wife washed out yer scarf." He gave Jean the damp cloth. Once they were moving, she'd hold it out the window. Getting in he offered change to her.

She shook her head. "You'll need gas and oil. Wait and give me what's left later."

"Said ah lost a heap a blood. Sez good thang ah'm s' healthy."

130

He put the bills in his breast pocket. "Told 'im 's what comes a not livin' in t' city. If ah was, be like t' rest a them folks. A-goin t' seed. Said when ah git home, 'bout a week, have m' doc t' take out t' stitches. Sez ah's lucky didn't cut no nerves. 'Twas a mite deep. Took fifteen stitches.

"You're some guy," Jean said. She saw he liked the way she said it.

He drove to the main street finding a gas station at the end of it. "Jean," he said softly.

"Yes?"

"Want y' t' he'p me with m' shirt. I'll put on 'nother time we leave here."

"Sure," she answered, undoing his buttons. Reaching around his shoulders taking away the cloth, her fingers touched his skin, felt the warmth and firmness of his body. She held his arm, guiding his hand through the short sleeve.

He told her, "Thank y'," looking boyish, his mouth, his eyes. She nodded slowly, and then rolled up the shirt and kept it under her hand.

Everyone used the rest rooms, washing and all, while the attendant filled the tank. When Johnny came back, he dug another shirt out of his maze in the trunk. And after he paid the bill, he asked Jean to give him a hand with it. Happy to help him, behind his back she smiled. In the washroom Kid could have done it.

While they were moving, she made sandwiches and passed them around. Sitting in back, Kid was quiet. He held his food for a number of miles before taking a nibble. That stuck in his throat. "Ah know yer mad at me, Johnny," he said.

The man said, "Ah ain't."

"Tell by the way y' act."

"Ain't, ah tell y'." He didn't give any advice.

131

Kid ate the sandwich then. It was gone soon. "Y' still gon teach me t' drive, Johnny?" He wheedled.

"Shore. Said ah was."

"You know he must've cared about you, taking your side like he did, grabbing that other boy," Jean sent back.

"Didn't grab 'im s' hard counta Kid," Johnny drawled. "Even after the fool thang he done, didn't aim t' see 'im git hisse'f hurt. S' jest when ah seed t' way 'at feller shoved y', doggone it made me s' mad."

"Is that right, Johnny?" she asked in a whisper.

He nodded. "Cain't stand t' see no man hit no woman. 'N' 'at boy's 'most a man. Did he hurtcha?"

"No, not really," she answered.

" 'S one thang m' first wife an t' woman ah'm married to now c'n say. Ah never hit 'im. 'S truth."

"Were they very much alike?" Jean wanted to know.

"Naw. Ellen Mae—we's married when ah's nineteen an' she's sixteen. We's t'gether five years. An' she's all time on me. But come a time ah seed we couldn't make it."

"She fussed a lot, huh?"

"Yep. Ever' day ah's ther. Sez she needed me at home."

"You mean she wanted you to do repairs?"

"Naw, warn't that. See, ah been goin' wher ah please since ah's a boy. Cain't set still too long. When ah feel like goin', ah go." He fought looking bitter. "She's a good woman but reckon she ain't never understood nothin' 'bout me, 'n' why ah got t' go like ah do. Ain't no two ways."

"What about the one you're married to now?" asked Jean.

"Good woman."

"What's her name?"

"Linda."

"How long have you been married?"

132

"Near four years. She's same age 's me. Twenty-eight."

"You're seven years older 'n I am," Jean told him.

"Yer twenty-one?"

"Mm-hm . . . Ever take your wife with you? Since you first got married, I mean." Jean had the arm nearest him folded over the top of the seat.

He shook his head. "She's all time askin'. But ah tell 'er naw. She never said nothin' . . . 'Cept this last time."

"What'd you say then?"

"Ah sez naw." Slowly. "She sez, Johnny, ah want t' go with y'. Ah don't want y' t' go an' leave me here. An' ah sez if ah'd of wanted y', ah'd of invited y'. Jest like 'at." He didn't sound mean.

"My goodness," said Jean.

" 'N' she sez when're y' comin' home? An' ah told 'er, gittin' in m' car, be back d'rectly." He grinned lightly, not letting out his feelings.

"And you've been away four months."

" 'S right."

"When you get back home, think she'll be there?"

"Shore," he said confidently. "Most likely have m' supper ready, bed all made."

Suddenly he didn't want to talk anymore about that. "Got t' rest a while," he said showing his hand.

Jean asked, "It hurts a lot?"

"Yep." Near Aspen they stopped. There were deep lines in his forehead. His throat moved. "Sonabitch!" He blurted out. "Sonabitch!" Panting, gulping, working his fingers. Closing his eyes then, he pressed his chin against his chest and let his arm dangle inward across one leg. "Sonabitch!" Swallowing, "Sonabitch, sonabitch, sonabitch!" Off and on for a minute or more while the others sat, quiet. Then he turned toward the girl and told her, "Ah had t' git it out. Cain't drive ner nothin'."

133

"I understand," she said softly.

Seeing the look she gave him, some of the fire went out of his hand, and he laid it on the steering wheel again, dwelling on the campsite. Sundown was cooling the sky and coloring the west. "Be ther 'fore dark, this place ah's tellin y' 'bout. C'n y' cook?" He was grinning now.

"Sure," she said. "What'll you have, roast turkey and cranberry sauce?"

"Weiners 'n' canned beans, ah reckon," he chuckled.

Sweet air came through the windows, scents off the evergreens. A few slow falls and rises later, in a place where the tall, timeless trees had thickened, they jogged right off the lonely strip onto a black dirt trail. Johnny followed the narrow curve to where four wooden tables stood together. Except for three smaller deciduous trees lending shade, a grassy area of about sixty yards in any direction was cleared. One outhouse welcomed on the left. And a water pipe with a spigot on top rose up a good bit right of center. With the car standing still, Johnny stretched grandly, arching his back and putting his hand behind his head. "Guess we c'n git out. Ah'll make a far," he was talking to Jean, "an yew 'n' Kid c'n he'p find some kindlin'."

"Won't hurt your hand, will it?" she asked.

He said, "Naw." Looked around. "Don't seem like it rained none here."

"No, it doesn't," she agreed, accepting the woods. "Brrr." She grabbed herself by the arms. "Chilly. Better get my jacket. Kid, hand it to me, please. It's right behind you." He did that for her. She struggled into it. "Mm, better." Then he wriggled out, like Johnny, in a T-shirt and khaki pants, not minding, and went after armfuls of the copious dry branches. She bobbed around the haven, sorting out such and laying it near Johnny who shaped some of it into a proper pile for burning. After some minutes of

134

running shuttle, she went back to the car and took out his rolled-up shirt, and got her own soiled clothing and soap, asking him, "Anything you want washed?"

He grinned, his face lighting, "Reckon." Raiding his trunk, he filled her arms. "Show y' somethin'," he said, taking out a large piece of plastic and a small spade. "Kid, come 'ere." The boy got in step, going toward the spout. When they were there, Johnny told him, "Want y' t' dig a hole 'bout this big." In the air he measured one the size of a small tub. And so the boy spaded fresh earth beneath the spout's mouth and, on quiet orders, fitted the flexible plastic into it letting the excess spread beyond it. Then Johnny turned the spigot forcing out a flood. "Ther y' are," he said finally.

"Pretty smart," Jean said, and put the clothes in, several pieces at a time, and fought out the dirt.

"Do mine too?" Kid pushed while the man went to work on the fire.

"I'll leave the plastic so you can do your own," Jean told him, not using her best voice.

" 'S all right. Ruther not," he came out glumly. For a time, he stood there studying Jean's soapy hands making stain come out of Johnny's shirt, with his hands in his pockets as far as the second knuckle, and hunched in a sail-in-the-wind pose. His lips were in a pout leaving great space for his stare. Once he reached up with a fist and conquered an itch on his nose. "What ah done t' 'at other feller back 'er? Ain't t' worst thang ah ever done."

"Don't tell me you're bragging?" she protested, standing up and forcing out rinsing water.

"That warn't nothin'. Done 'way worse 'n 'at one time."

"Well, keep it to yourself. I don't want to hear it," she said, disgusted. He stood near her for a space while she hung some of the clothes on branches, then went to where the fire was beginning to rise.

When she finished and some of the trees were semaphoring gently, she pulled out the transparent stopper, rinsed it, and shook it. Brilliant little blobs flew. Some wet her face. She saw midget wetness cover the front of her jacket. By the time she had hung that up, the earth had taken back half the water. She forced out the rest by filling the crater with the small loam hill beside it. Johnny looked so far away stooping near the blaze. Steadily he grew larger. "Hey, Captain," she said, "ready for a good cook yet?"

He liked that and it showed in his eyes when he looked up. "Reckon. Kid, git t' vittles out t' car." The boy was there and back again, not sensing what to bring from either bag or that he might make a choice, or at least ask what special things the others wanted. Without cues he didn't exist. Except as a goblin. Obeying took two trips.

"Ooookay, let's see what's what," she sighed, rubbing her hands before the fire.

"Much 'bliged t' y' fer washin' m' clothes," Johnny told her.

"You're welcome," she said, taking out packages and putting them on the nearest table.

She made salad on a paper plate, and got out the buns, chips, and salt. And on his buddy's say-so, Kid pricked two cans of beans, heated them on hot rocks planted in the flames, and found sticks for the frankfurters. There were logs for sitting. Waiting for the beans, Kid and Jean peeled the sticks. Jean had two. "Johnny, let's sang somethin'," Kid suggested, sitting three yards away from the man on the other side of the fire.

"Whatcha want t' sang?" the other asked.

Kid pondered. "How 'bout 'Kentucky Wonder'?"

"Know that un, Jean?" Johnny questioned.

"Afraid I don't," she answered, fixing a frank on a long stick and giving it to him.

He tucked it under his armpit and held it in place on embers with his knee and wrist. "Y' c'n ketch onta it," he promised.

> "She's m'long Kentucky wonder.
> Green an' tender when ah bend 'er—"

It was peppy. Jean struggled along, trying the tune and at the same time hooking meat to her own wand. Kid managed to burn up his and had to get another.

The song went on haunting the darkening hollow in plaintive southern Indiana style. She went to the table. She divided the salad on other paper circles, put buns, chips, forks on each. The beans were ready, so she opened the cans and added those. Johnny was given the one with the most. He was grateful, putting it on one knee and letting her take his stick and free the meat. "Lay it right t'er on the beans." He got satisfaction. And she opened three bottles of soda then, and riffled out two.

As Kid got his fare from her hands, he sent no messages, and gulped it down in an unfriendly hurry. That aggravated Jean. Until she looked at him again, forking food into his string-of-a frame. He'd been hungry for a long time. A little ashamed, she sat down beside Johnny and dipped into her own, the smallest plate.

The meal tasted extra good with the flavor of the woods in it. Everybody had seconds. Night fell. The fire warmed doubly. There was plenty of kindling. The boy and the man sat with their legs apart, except that Johnny had his knees bent. They moaned other songs. And relishing it all, Jean listened. Until they weren't singing anymore. Just sitting there poking up sparks and savoring the night smells.

137

"Wanted t' do this a-fore. Never had no chance," said Johnny.

"Fun, isn't it?" she sent back.

"Yep. Kinda friendly too, cookin' out."

"By the way, that was a good idea, digging that hole," she said.

"Doin' fer m'se'f here 'n' there, differ'nt thangs come t' me."

"Johnny's smart," Kid said. "Even made 'is car."

Jean said, "You didn't?"

Johnny shifted his forehead. "Ah did."

"From scratch?"

"Yep. Mostly. Got sheet metal and sich. Old parts. Course she stops some, like y' seed."

"That's wonderful," she murmured. Kid saw the man grin.

"Oh, reckon ther's some others could do that."

"Johnny," she whispered, enjoying his face, "where'd you learn that?"

"Watchin' other folks. Ennythang ah see, study it fer a minute er ask someone t' show me, ah'll larn it. Don't take me no time. Got me a auto repair shop in Longview. Everybody knows me. Time ah git back, open up, folks'll be brangin' in ther cars fer me t' fix."

Left out, Kid whined, "'S mite cold. Thank ah'll go set in t' car."

"Git one a them blankets," Johnny suggested.

"Naw. Reckon ah'll sleep some." He threw his empty plate into the fire.

"Sleep on t' table."

"Naw." He went away.

138

Chapter Fourteen

Johnny dragged wood onto the bright heat and stirred things up with his forked stick. "Tell me about Vincennes," she asked him.

"It's real nice," he said. "Got good folks ther."

"Your mother, what's she like?"

He chuckled, "Fat. Say me 'n' her got t' same face. Sez ah's 'er fav'rite. Never could tell it. Ah's a kid, she's all time fussin' at me."

"And what'd you do then?"

"Jest go off some'ers by m'se'f. Mostly t' place name of Sugar Loaf. 'At's a ole Injun mound. Say the Shawnee used t' hold ther cer'monies right t'er." He told her about sitting watching squirrels, rabbits. Anything to keep from going home. "R'member back a ways yew's talkin 'bout them gulls an' childern's drawin's?"

"Yes."

"Well, one time they's 'is bird a-settin' on ole Sugar Loaf. It 'uz a big un. Never seed nothin' like it a-fore er since. Eyes jest as sharp, 's proud an' strong. Ah kept a-watchin' it. An' 'en it hopped up an' flied off." He put his head down, poking the fire once, twice, taking a breath. "Tried m' best t' foller it . . . Come

139

home late. Told m' mother. She never knowed what 'twas. Sez ah's tellin' a tale. Ah sez naw."

"What was it, Johnny?" the girl asked, feeling the heat and the shadows and seeing the side of his face.

"Ole Jess Bruner lived next door. One used t' sang 'at song?" He went over the words. She remembered. "He come 'bout then. Ah told 'im what ah seed. Sez sounds like a ole eagle. Ain't none a them 'round these parts. Ah sez knowed what ah seed."

"How old were you?" Jean asked.

"Eight. 'Most nine."

"You were sort of little to be wandering all over the place."

He put his head even lower, then looked up. "Ah's never little. Thirteen ah's big 's ah am now. Looked jest 's old. Did a man's work."

She thought about that, then asked, "Did your mother ever believe you?"

He sent his head back and forth, lowering his eyes. "She kept a-sayin' ah wasn't tellin' the truth. Got 'er a switch an' whupped me. Sez don't y' go out ther no more. Jest t' same ah kept a-goin' . . . Knowed ah seed 'at ole bird. Ah's intendin' t' ketch it an' take it home an' show ever'one so 's 'ey could see ah wasn't tellin' no tale."

"Was it ever there after that?"

He frowned gently, looked off. "Never no more." And the woods grew still. Something moved on dry branches somewhere among the trees, too weakly to frighten. Tiny fires soared and died. And Jean waited, one hand palm up on the other. Johnny was talking again. "Ever time ah'd leave home m' mother sez ah's goin' after 'at ole eagle." He thrust his stick against the fire. Then a little smile showed. He sighed and raised his forehead, making wrinkles. "She told me that when ah's home this time." He raked a coal. "Been goin' since ah's sixteen. 'At's t' first ah

140

ever stayed away." Clearing his throat, he let the sound left in him wait, breathing more, remembering.

She asked, "Where'd you go?"

" 'Cross Illinois, down inta Kansas . . . Got a job in a sawmill. Worked two months. M' daddy's dead. M' mother's takin' in washin'. Wasn't much money comin' in."

"What about your sisters?

"Had ther own fam'lies. Figgered ah'd work a while 'n' save what ah made an' go back an he'p out some." He plastered his lips against his teeth and she heard him inhale hard. Then his mouth opened a slit. " 'At's wher ah lost m' arm. One a them saws cut 't off."

"Oh, my God," Jean gasped, showing pain but no pity. She knew he wouldn't tolerate pity.

"Never even yelled. Didn't make no noise atall."

"Oh, God! . . . What did they do about it? Didn't they give you any insurance coverage or compensation?"

"Nothin'," Johnny said grimly, his face not hiding his feelings. And then as if that did no good, said lamely, "Foreman claimed ah's too young t' be workin' ther. Sez they wasn't gittin' in no trouble counta me. An' ah went on back home." He stopped jabbing the hot pile and put his hand on his knee and leaned back against the table and closed his eyes.

"How could they be that cruel?" Jean managed, holding back too late tears.

"Been a fer piece since then. Been all over. 'Most enny state y' c'n name. Alaska—" his jaw grew hard. "But ah always worked m' way. Don't take nothin' from nobody fer nothin'. Give 'em the best job ah c'n ennyplace ah go." He frowned and his mouth worked, leaving certain words in his heart. "An' after m' arm was cut off, didn't want t' do nothin' ner talk t' nobody—jest—ah don't know." He waited again, moving his fingers, the firelight

141

on him, " 'N' 'en ole Jess Bruner sez, Son—all time called me Son—reckon no one knows how y' feel. Sez ah'm gon tell y' somethin'. Drag yer feet an' y' dig yer own grave. Ain't no sense stumblin' through life. Ever'day y' got t' walk like a man. Do a man's work. 'S what he told me. Never did fergit it, neither." He scratched his upright hair while the stars slid on to an appointed place in the sky. He turned to face her. "Don't talk t' folks much—'bout m'se'f ner nothin' deep. What ah told y' ain't said t' nobody don't already know. Kinda like talkin' t' y'." He saw her eyes light up and her full lips part, then moved his fingers on her palm. "Y' got soft hands. Ther gentle. Noticed when y' tied on 'at bandage. Ought t' be a nurse."

"Okay. And when I get my car," she promised, "I'll let you fix it."

Some of the past had gone away from his mood. He said, "Guess Kid's a-sleepin'."

"Must've been half dead," Jean said. "He sure looks up to you."

He grinned. "Ah reckon. Tries t' be jest like me. Wears 'is hair 'most like ah do. He ast 'is mother if he could come with me. Knowed 'im from a baby. Held 'im in m' arms."

"You were pretty young yourself," she said. He let that ride up with the luminous dust on the barely moving wind. They sat closer now, in a small way touching. "It's getting late. Better throw away the trash and get ready for bed." The wire basket was outside the periphery of flickering light.

"Go with y' t' protect y'," he intoned and smiled a little. They sailed their plates into the flames and got up. She collected throwaways. Together they walked away from the fire and into the dark.

"Here 'tis," she said, freeing the stuff for descent.

"Wait," he told her softly, "let's walk over by them trees."

Where it was darker. From where they could see the fire without being seen, the way it barely lit the car. Its flame was low and even, strange without them, and strange the empty logs, the unoccupied tables, the great exciting quiet pungent with pine. He put the tips of his fingers on her cheek, warmth and strength moving. "It's s' soft," feeling the fire under her hair. Staring, she could make out the charged margin of his face, hear and feel his power. She reached up and caressed his temple, and he sensed her trembling and waiting. His arm enclosed her willingness under her jacket. She went to him, swelling against his heartbeat, pressed to him throat to thigh. His mouth searched down to hers and she yielded. Then he whispered, "Ah wanted t' fer s' long, seein' y' next t' me."

She clung to him, murmured, "Oh, Johnny," and they kissed, kissed, swelling, craving.

Drowning in light!

They weren't together anymore.

The accusation fell to a puny circle on the ground. Kid stood shock-still, staring at the two of them. Johnny grunted, agitated, "Whatcha doin' over here? Thought yew's 'sleep?" Knowing now that he and Jean had been watched leaving the campfire, had been heard every step of the way because the trees volleyed the sound.

"Ah-ah had t' go piss."

"Outhouse's over t' other side," Johnny told him steadily.

Kid dropped his head for a second. "Got mixed up." Jean stood silent.

"Well, guess y' c'n go on now, huh?" The man advised coolly.

"Guess ah better," Kid shot back meanly, his head up, " 'fore m' prick leaks all over everthang!"

"Oh, for goodness sake," Jean came out. "Do you have to say and do everything that comes into your head?"

He grumbled through a tight mouth, "Ain't nothin'. Like ah's tellin' y' a-fore, only y' wouldn't let me. Did way worse 'n 'at one time."

"I don't want to hear it." Fuming, she jammed her hands into her jacket pockets.

"Why don'tcha go 'n' do whatcha gotta do?" Johnny nudged.

The little light shook. "Did somethin' a whole lot worse even 'n spittin' on 'at feller."

"Kid," said Johnny.

Puffing hard. "Ah screwed a calf once."

"Ugh!" Jean gasped, turning backward. Johnny held his ground.

"Ain't 'shamed."

Jean spun back to face the boy, making fists at her sides. "Why—" she nearly shouted—"don't you have some *pride?*"

Kid caved in in the middle. The light went out. He took two steps away from the man and the woman, then ran following the dark somewhere. Not long afterward, they heard the outhouse door squeak, bang repeatedly before it was still again. "Let's go over to the fire," she sighed.

"If y' want."

"Think we'd better." Close in another way, they didn't touch.

There were only embers. "Ain't too cold. Guess we won't need this t'night," the man decided.

She said, "Guess not."

"Don't thank he's bad ner nothin' like 'at. Jest come up hard, same's me. No daddy 'n'—hard."

"Is he really seventeen?" she quivered, feeling one table to see if it was solid.

"Yep."

"But he's not going into the army, is he?"

144

Johnny's exhaling made embers glow. "Naw. Cain't read ner write. He jest made that up."

It didn't do any good telling him he ought to have some pride, she was thinking. But I had to say it. Someone should've a long time ago. The horizontal board didn't budge, the legs were sturdy. "Blankets in the trunk?" she asked out loud.

"Yep. Want me t' git 'em?"

"No. I'll bring yours too and put the food away." She made a quick trip. The cavity was already unlocked and partly open. She unloaded half the bedding on another tabletop, then began making her bed.

A frail silhouette trod toward the car. "Night, Kid," the man called out. He got no answer. He gazed until the door opened and closed, and let it go at that.

The spot that had blazed once was dying under dirt. And she asked, "Johnny, whenever you go someplace—all those years I mean—" she had his attention—"you always get around to seeing your family, don't you?"

He said, "Shore."

"Well, suppose you went to visit your mother and she wasn't there."

"Aw, she's all time home. She don't go nowhere."

"But let's say maybe next time she wasn't. And then when you got down to Alabama, the place was locked up. And then in Texas you found they'd gone away."

"Wouldn't hardly be like 'at."

"I'm just saying. What if you went home to Longview and your house was dark and empty. Or worse, say there was a 'For Rent' sign on it? What then, Johnny?" No answer. "Would it be okay? I mean for someone else to take a notion to be gone besides you?"

"Don't know," he pondered. "Kinda like havin' them ther when ah git ther."

"I know. But that's what I'm trying to say. You want them there, but what if they want you? What if your wife, say—needs you? And you're not there?"

"Aw, she's healthy."

"You don't know what could happen. The house could burn down one night or robbers could come. Johnny, you're never around to know." His mouth moved once or twice. "You call whenever you get a notion—maybe every month or so. Lot could go wrong between calls. And she not able to reach you."

Johnny walked to where Jean was and said, "Y' don't thank much a me, do y'?"

"Is that the way I sound?" she whispered, looking up at him. "You're so wrong." For a moment she looked at the stars. "Oh, I don't know why I'm acting this way. Telling you how to run your life." She sat on the nearest table and put her feet on the bench. "What're we doing out here, Johnny?"

"Y' mean t'gether?" he wondered.

"No, I mean what're we doing out here at all? This going, trying to get somewhere."

"Sometimes ah thank thataway," said Johnny. "Sometimes when it's s' cold er stormin' s' bad like it was a-fore—" smoke came up in threads—"er ah'm s' hungry. An' feel like ah'm no more 'n a speck a-lookin' up at all 'at sky. And land's fer 's ah c'n see."

"That's what we are. Specks," she answered. "Dust on the road, blowing to wherever. How long?" She waited but not for an answer and then said, "The sun's going to come up and catch us."

"Sayin' goodnight, huh?"

"I guess."

146

He leaned toward her and kissed her on the cheek. For an instant only she held his face, felt his body touching hers, then leaned away and left the table. "Say, we could bunk in t' same place," he offered.

She laughed softly, "Let's don't."

"So ah c'n protect y'."

"Night, Johnny."

"Er we could shove two a these tables side b' side."

"Johnny—dear Johnny—night."

Full of good nature, he stretched to his feet and went to look after the other blankets. "Healthy fer y', sleepin' out like 'is," he told her.

She answered, "That's what they say."

"Be in Portland t'morra afte'noon."

"No time at all . . . Pleasant dreams."

"Ah won't snore ner nothin'."

"Good," she said, smiling in the dark.

Chapter Fifteen

Jean got up first and tortured herself at the pump, shivering clean before Johnny sat up to the morning. She waved and took things out of the trunk and then hid among the trees. Birds chirped. Water splashed again. She peered out and saw Johnny nude to the waist in a crouch wetting his skin. A feeling held from the night forever gone filled her, and she wondered what it would be like being with him past Portland, down the years, and sighed. How could she? Or any woman? She pitied his wife, envying her.

Sunlight shone on the green clearing. Midget noises rustled the near places. There was wood still beside the ashes. By the time she had settled her feelings and went over to take the clothes off the boughs, Johnny had a fire leaping. "How'd y' sleep?" he asked, holding a clean tan T-shirt belt high on his levis and seeing her in a blouse and skirt with her hair hanging loose.

"Like you said, it's healthy. How about you?"

"Fine."

"Want me to help you with your shirt?"

" 'Preciate it." In soft, gentle seconds he was fully dressed. "Guess ah better git Kid up. Be ther time t' go. *Kid! Yo Kid!*"

"I'll get breakfast ready," Jean said, walking, arms loaded, toward the table.

"Kid!"

"Y-yep?"

"C'mon. Time t' git to it. 'S daylight 'n' then some."

" 'Kay." Inside the car a head rose up, rumpled. A hand scratched on top. Kid opened the door and wandered out, still wearing sleep. He engineered his mouth open, scrawled disorder between his eyes, erased it, and saw the others.

"Mornin'," Johnny said casually.

The boy said, "Mornin'."

"Morning," Jean said.

"Mornin'." Kid went to the john. After that he washed up and wet his hair down.

Taking out food, she followed the boy's pallid approach, him holding his shirt in his hand exposing his loins to tepid air. He dug a clean white shirt out of the mobile cache, discarding the dirty one and buttoning himself back to order. The goblin cast was gone. She couldn't guess what he had on his mind. While she readied breakfast, he traced the edge of the clearing a step at a time. "Meant t' tell y', y' look right perty," the man told the woman. "Kinda like y' in a skirt."

"Thought I would since we'll be in Portland soon," she lied.

"Don't mind what ah said last night."

"All right."

"But ah meant it. Wasn't jest tryin' y' out."

She smiled then. "I hoped you weren't."

"Wasn't s' shore y' liked me."

"I do. A lot."

He grinned. "Ah was uncommon eager."

"Tell you a secret. So was I."

"Was it Kid?"

"Partly," she admitted. "And when I had a chance to think, it's only been two days, and there won't be any more. After Portland, I'll never see you again."

"Come on t' Longview." He sounded sincere.

She sighed, "Oh, Johnny"—laughed a little—"maybe one day. And probably you'll be gone somewhere else. Besides, it wouldn't work out. But I can remember you and that's a lot." She poured cereal into paper cups. "What you said last night about dragging your feet—"

"Yep?"

"I didn't go to sleep right away thinking about that. And how I'd been in a rut hating everybody. Now I don't. Oh, I'm not suddenly in love with the world. Some folks I'll never get along with. Only it got to the point where even when folks were nice, I still hated them. Nice wasn't enough. It took more. You. The way you are." She wanted to touch him, but didn't. Kid was close to closing his circle.

And back again he sat on his log with stingy air between his knees, his shoulders hunched a bit. Jean gave out full plates and cups. Johnny thanked her, feeling good about what she'd told him.

"You're welcome," she answered, and served Kid.

"He took what she had for him, mumbling, "Thank y'."

Surprised, she acknowledged that. And they all battled gnats and ate.

Soon, they were rolling out of the clearing. And except for warm ashes, no one could tell they had been there. Sitting by himself, Kid gave up talking. Jean heard the warm wind moaning of dead mines and ghost towns and old wars through old things growing and kin to them all. And it troubled her sadness, the wind, the wind.

While they pulled up the hill, at Johnny's request she turned on the radio, bringing in music. And several songs later, they were in Boise. Johnny said, "Well, won't be long. We c'n git gas here."

"And let's find the bus depot," she sighed.

He nodded slowly. The boy shifted around in back, and Johnny asked, "Y' all right, Kid?"

"Yep." Softly.

"Thought yew's sick. Y' ain't sayin' nothin'."

"Got nothin' t' say."

"Don't seem like y'." Johnny didn't bother him after that. "Guess m' wife'll be a-settin' out front keepin' 'er eyes on the road lookin' fer me," he said to Jean. She didn't answer. "What y' told me 'bout goin' all time? Made up m' mind ah'm gon do differ'nt. Know it ain't gon be easy."

"You mean you'll stop roaming?"

"In a way. Stay home long 's ah c'n. An when ah go, it won't be fer s' long. An' ah'll phone a heap more t' see how everthang is, let m' wife know wher ah'll be."

"Why don't you take her with you?"

"Thought 'bout that. Might. But ah figger better do it gradual. A-fore long, settle down . . . She's a good woman. Give 'er trouble, ah reckon."

At a filling station, he learned from the attendant where the depot was. Half a block down, on the right side of the street. Couldn't miss it. Johnny set his car in slow motion, went a little way, and stopped.

"White Hare Bus Lines," Jean read out loud.

"Hold on," Johnny said. "Y' got change comin'."

"I'll get it when I come back," she told him, going into a plain little hotel.

A tall man at the room service desk said the fare from Boise was twenty-nine, fifty-five. From Portland it was twenty dollars even. Jean went outside again. Johnny was frowning. "I'm going with you to Portland," she told him quietly, and saw him smile.

When she got in beside him again, he put bills and coins in her hand. "Pay y' back ever' cent," he insisted.

"You don't have to," she said. "Let's just say you've got the car, and I got the fuel."

"Nope."

"But, Johnny—"

"Ah'm gon pay y' back . . . Soon 's we git t' Portland, ah'm gon call m' mother in Vincennes. Tell 'er t' wire some money. Ah kept a count a how much . . . She knows ah'm good fer it. Allus was."

"You don't have to."

"Ah wanta."

Somewhere along the way, he told her, "One time ah's in Oklahoma City an' ah seed this one-arm man a-standin' on a street corner beggin'. Ah went up t' him an' sez, y' damn no good sonuvabitch, ah'm a one-arm man jest like yew. An' yew don't have t' beg. 'S what ah told 'im." Anger scalded him, looking back.

"What did he say?" she asked, amazed and noticing how differently he said the curseword.

"Stood ther with 'is mouth open. Skeered 'im, ah guess. But it made me s' mad. Almost hit 'im. But ah didn't . . . Ther's times ah've hit a man . . . Defendin' m'se'f . . . Never hit no woman, like ah said . . . Kicked m' wife outa bed once." He looked serious.

"What in the world for?"

"Didn't go t' do it. Ah's 'sleep. Dreamin'. An' first thang ah knowed, she's a-sayin', 'Johnny, whatcha kick me fer?' She's a-lyin' on t' floor. Ah sez, 'Woman, git back in t' bed. Didn't know ah kicked y'.'" He grinned slowly, seeming far from his former

152

distress. "Told 'er ah's sorry." It was the way he was. Changing in seconds. Or at least he seemed to change. Keeping things buried under his good humor. Millions of miles of hurts and wants. Feelings that she knew were full and powerful. Except, every once in a while, some of it bulged out, good humor be damned.

The road stretched little more than eighty miles from Boise to Portland. Passing larch and ponderosa, the radio played on. "Won't be long," Johnny mentioned. "Hey, Kid, be in Longview time fer supper, jest like ah said." No answer. "Makes y' feel good, don't it?"

"Guess he doesn't feel like talking anymore," Jean said.

"Ah'm jest doin' like y' told me . . . Havin' some pride!" That last word had all the hurt in it.

She saw him defensive and wistful then, said in a murmur, "Meant to tell you, you look nice, Kid."

He fingered the collar of his short-sleeved shirt and looked down. His mouth softened, saying, "Thank y'."

Leaving Idaho, they crossed the Snake River. "In Oregon now," the blond man said. Said again, "Won't be long."

"Won't be long," she repeated, wanting to touch him.

And then the ride ended.

"Better git yer thangs outa the trunk," Johnny said. She nodded. "Kid, y' c'n stay in t' car if y' like 'til ah git back." They were in front of the bus station, a drab old building.

"Ah'm comin' with y'," the boy told him. Johnny unlocked the steel rump. Kid reached inside without fervor and said, "Ah'll git it." The man and the woman smiled at each other.

Inside the building Jean said, "Better find the ticket windows first." Her voice broke.

"Look fer us by them phone booths," Johnny told her. "Gon call m' mother."

"You'll need a dime," she said, thinking that he looked out of place in the city.

He said, "Got one."

Leaving her bag with them, she wandered off to one of the long lines facing small windows that framed men's faces. After a short wait, she had her ticket and was asking, "What time does the next bus leave?"

Reading his watch, the man said soberly, "Loading in ten minutes."

She left the window, hurrying by other travelers, and found Kid guarding her bag near the second booth on her right. Johnny was inside, holding the receiver to his ear. "Been callin' an' callin'," he drawled, worried. Now and then the ringing pulsed in his forehead. "Cain't understand. She ain't never out this time a day." In Vincennes it was minutes after six.

"My bus comes pretty soon. It's okay, hear, Johnny?"

"Naw. Know ah c'n git 'er."

"It doesn't matter."

He let the ringing stop. "Ah'll try his house. Maybe she's over ther. Lives next door. What's 'at number?" Kid told him. The man braced the phone between his jaw and shoulder. Jean heard the coin fall, and then the sound of dialing. Then ringing . . . And ringing . . . Showing in his eyes . . . "They never go out this time a day . . . Gotta be ther . . . Ah don't understand."

"Johnny—my bus—look—please—it was a favor to me, believe me, please—" She was losing control of herself.

"Maybe ah got t' wrong number," he said, stunned and humili-ated. "Wait, 'fore y' go. One time. Jest let me try one time."

With her eyes closed and her hand over her mouth, she was crying. "You don't understand—you don't see—Johnny—"

Frantically, "Wait! 'Nother minute. They got t' be home! Not both a 'em gone!" And the ringing in his eyes.

154

"Bus now loading at gate 24 for Jlkopwjfnvkt, Smcnvfogy, Dhnaz Uyrtge, and San Francisco!"

"I'll miss my bus," she whispered and reached for her bag.

"Don't go jest yit. Look. Y' c'n take 'nother one. Later ah c'n most likely git 'em."

"It doesn't matter, don't you see? Thanks, you hear? So much."

He gave up the phone. Another man was waiting for it. Right away he made a connection. "They's allus ther," Johnny gagged, showing pain.

"Bye, Johnny."

"Ah tried t' git 'em but ah cain't." He put the dime in her hand.

Her fingers closed around the feel of his fingers. "I know," she told him. Tears streamed down her cheeks. "Bye, Kid." The boy raised his hand weakly. Feeling terrible, she hurried away.

People were blurred, clustering for travel. Bumping into some, she apologized. The station was a cold barn, full of noise.

Then, "Jean! Wait!" Johnny was running after her. Holding back tears, she stopped bare yards from the San Francisco line. He took her bag from her, gripping it under his arm. "Told Kid t' stay ther," he said and walked with her.

"Your hand," she whispered.

"Don't feel it s' much. Jest come t' me yew's leavin'." The bad feeling was still there and something more. "Thought ah'd see y' got on t' right bus . . . Hope y' ain't thankin' hard a me 'cause a the money."

"I don't care about it. I mean it."

He knew she did, saying, "Hope everthang works out fer y'. Down in California."

"What could happen to me?" she came out, struggling to be pleasant.

"Well, jest t' same . . . It's all over s' quick," he said, talking low.

She saw how warm his eyes were. "I'll never forget you," she told him, "not ever." The tears were coming again. She tried to smile. "And every time I see an eagle—" she saw herself in his eyes.

By then the bus was half loaded. He stood beside her until she handed over her ticket. The tears had been wiped away. A man in a red cap gave her a check for her luggage. Johnny said, "Good luck, y' hear?"

"You too," she told him.

When the bus pulled out, he was still standing on the platform. She could see him through the window, his bandaged hand high, and sent up her own hand until she couldn't see him anymore.

Chapter Sixteen

"Crescent City," said the driver entering California. "No," Jean hadn't any oranges—

though by nightfall she had a room. And a job in two weeks. She called Chris then, had to talk to her no matter how it turned out.

And Chris said, "Jeannie! Honey, how are you?" As if nothing had happened.

"I'm okay. You?"

"Just fine. You're in San Francisco?"

"Uh-huh."

"It's so good to hear your voice."

"Good hearing yours, Chris. I've started working again."

"That's wonderful. Doing what?"

"Clerk in a department store. Just like in Chicago."

"Oh, Bernie's going to be tickled you're doing so well."

As if nothing had happened.

"How is he?" Casually.

"Girl, he's painting the house outside. Had to go to the store and get some more thinner. He'll be so sorry he missed you. And

157

I've been dieting and doing a little housecleaning and what not since you left."

"That's nice. I'm glad."

"By the way, there's a letter for you. From someone named Ferris Boone."

Jean was hot all of a sudden. "Oh? When did it come?"

"About five days ago." She said he'd called the day after Jean left. That he got their name through information. "Talked with him a good while. Told him you'd been here. He's got a nice voice."

Jean's temples ticked. "Yes, he has. What's the letter say?"

"Oh, I didn't open it. Says please forward on the envelope. I'll send it."

"No, read it, please."

There was a frustrating wait of paper rattling. The letter wasn't long. Ferris hated writing. Chris stumbled over some of his words—"has a job and he's going to stick with it this time." And wherever Jean was to call him collect. He was "cracking up" without her. Listening, Jean closed her eyes. He'd pay her fare back to Chicago so they could get married. Or come and get her. He loved her. A P.S. read that her things were still there and in good shape. "Want the number?"

Jean said, "I already know it."

"He sure sounds interested," said Chris, sounding like a big sister. "Let me know how it comes out."

And Jean told her, "Don't get your hopes up too soon." Chris asked her what she meant. "That's all. Just don't get your hopes up."

"All right. But either way, let me know. And, Jeannie—"

"Yes?"

"Forgive me, hear? I must've been—I was just feeling miserable and all upset—please forgive me."

158

"You don't have to ask. I love you," Jean said, smiling over the phone.

And Chris said, "That makes me feel so much better."

Though Jean knew she wasn't well. Not so soon. "Tell Bernie hi," she said.

"I will." Jean and her sister shared good-byes.

No, she couldn't be well yet. "I called at the right time," she said to herself, overjoyed that she had. She put the phone down.

And Ferris wanted to get married.

She sprawled across the bed, weak, seeing the flat shade covering the light in the ceiling. She thought about Johnny then, wondered what he was doing. Johnny. She didn't even know his last name.

Ferris! Wanted her!

Well, she wasn't sure what she would decide about that.

But anyhow, she would call him.